A Bloody Good Friday

Desmond Barry was born and brought up in Wales. He moved to the United States in the mid-1980s and now lives in New Jersey. He works in Tibet during the summer and is presently an External Fellow of Glamorgan University. His first novel, *The Chivalry of Crime*, was voted Best First Novel of the Year by The Western Writers of America and was shortlisted for the Arts Council of Wales Book of the Year Award.

A BLOODY GOOD FRIDAY

DESMOND BARRY

Jonathan Cape
London

Published by Jonathan Cape 2002

2 4 6 8 10 9 7 5 3 1

First published in Great Britain in 2002 by
Jonathan Cape
Random House, 20 Vauxhall Bridge Road,
London SW1V 2SA

Random House Australia (Pty) Limited
20 Alfred Street, Milsons Point, Sydney,
New South Wales 2061, Australia

Random House New Zealand Limited
18 Poland Road, Glenfield,
Auckland 10, New Zealand

Random House (Pty) Limited
Endulini, 5A Jubilee Road, Parktown 2193, South Africa

The Random House Group Limited Reg. No. 954009

A CIP catalogue record for this book
is available from the British Library

ISBN 0–224–06201–8

Papers used by The Random House Group Limited are natural,
recyclable products made from wood grown in sustainable forests;
the manufacturing processes conform to the environmental
regulations of the country of origin

Typeset by Palimpsest Book Production Limited,
Polmont, Stirlingshire

Printed and bound in Great Britain by
Biddles Ltd, Guildford & King's Lynn

The setting for this novel is the town of Merthyr Tydfil, where I grew up. Some of the events and characters arise out of local legends and recent histories of various towns and cities in South Wales and relocated here. The names of pubs and churches have been changed. Let it be noted, however, that this story is fictitious and all thoughts and actions are entirely imaginary and meant to bear no resemblance to any persons living or dead.

A man that had six mortal wounds, a man
Violent and famous, strode among the dead;
Eyes stared out of the branches and were gone.

Then certain Shrouds that muttered head to head
Came and were gone. He leant upon a tree
As though to meditate on wounds and blood.

A Shroud that seemed to have authority
Among those bird-like things came, and let fall
A bundle of linen . . .

'Now must we sing and sing the best we can,
But first you must be told our character:
Convicted cowards all, by kindred slain

'Or driven from home and left to die in fear.'
They sang, but had nor human tunes nor words,
Though all was done in common as before;

They had changed their throats and had the throats
   of birds.

From *W.B. Yeats, 'Cuchulain Comforted'*

Chapter 1

1

If you want to know what really went on, on that violent Good Friday night, then you have to ask me, Davey Daunt, because I have tracked down all the survivors of those bloody encounters that erupted in April 1977 upon the narrow high street of the town of Merthyr Tydfil·and I have drunk with those men and women, boys and girls, in order to loosen their tongues; and I have wheedled and connived, lied and tricked in order to trip their stories out of their own mouths so that I might write it down, write it all down here, God's honest truth, which the tabloids and the so-called serious papers, and radio and television and police reports have all twisted into something hideous and unrecognisable, a tissue of lies and distortion. The stories of these witnesses, who were in every hot spot in town, I have coupled with the events that I saw with my own eyes on the night that my mate Macky was propelled into legend as he struck off at a catastrophic tangent from the maelstrom of riot.

Let us begin on the morning of that day.

Eight a.m.

Macky was released from Swansea Jail, and Melly

Saunders, a delightful woman with a lot of flesh on a small body, picked him up in her clattery Cortina and brought him back to Merthyr. She had thrown open her house for us all to celebrate his return and the party had already been going for about eight hours when I limped in on the one good leg and the other withered by polio, the old steel caliper hidden under my blue denim, bath-shrunk Levis. I was in party clothes: leather jacket over a clean white T-shirt, long ginger hair hanging like curtains around my face, forget the fucking safety pins and swastikas, I made my transition from freak to punk via the Ramones just like most of my mates, if indeed there had been any transition to make. You can judge for yourself on that account. But a time of transition it was.

I scanned Melly's little house with my baby blue eyes. It was packed: Big Morgan, Maria Grazia, Melly and her many female minions, and various hangers-on and sycophants who are not worth listing, for though they may have heard of Macky they only admired him from a safe distance. The air was full of smoke, heavy Afghani smoke, and I grabbed a flagon of Festival Vat from among the overflowing ashtrays on the coffee table and tipped to my lips that awful sour cider made from pears that will draw the moisture from your tongue and the sense from your senses. The thunder of some astounding rutting resounded through the tiny terraced house.

'Hiya, Davey,' Melly said.

'Where's Macky then?'

'Upstairs with Angela Griffiths,' she said.

Ah, that was the source of the noise. Macky and

Angela Griffiths. Fuck me. That stunning child goddess. Just the thought of her gave me a hard-on: so thin, with long blonde hair, no more than fourteen, a mere girl who maintained her waif-like looks through smoking long Dunhills and frequent indulgence in various narcotics known to be used by the models who shagged Mick Jagger. Macky, I suppose, was the closest thing that the town had to a rock star. He was famous all over the South Wales valleys as a fighter of policemen, skinheads, gypsies, all comers. And this waif had blessed the Mack by offering her body so that he could breach his prison abstinence.

God, what I wouldn't have done to get some of that.

Then across the crowd I saw Maria Grazia's gorgeous head with that thick dark shock of corkscrew hair. Coming towards me through the bodies, she was bent over her patchwork tote bag as she rummaged for a packet of Marlboros. Then she was actually standing next to me.

'Listen to them up there,' she said.

She was talking to *me*. I had pigeons in my chest. Fucking tumblers.

'Aye. Macky's got a lot of catching up to do,' I said.

'Davey Daunt, isn't it?' she said.

'Yeah. Maria Grazia, right? Nice to see you in the old town, like. Back for long, is it?'

She found her cigarettes and offered me one.

I shook my head. I hadn't smoked for ages but now I wished that I did — just to have another point of contact with her. She had this face like a chubby little doll, dark brown eyes lined with black and the cheeks rouged, a little full over the fine bones, a slight double chin. She seemed like she was nervous herself, maybe even intimidated by all these people with nasty reputations gathered in the same place and breathing the same smoky air.

'I'm back for a while,' she said. 'It didn't work out so well in Italy.'

I nodded. She knew that I knew, of course, because that's the way the town is. She put a cigarette between her dark lipsticked lips. I would have liked to have lit it for her but I didn't have any matches. She used a thin gold lighter that she dropped back in the tote bag. I hoped that none of the kleptomaniac guests had noticed the value of it.

'I heard you were a painter,' I said.

The rhythm upstairs was picking up. Ba Doom. Ba Doom. Ba Doom.

She cocked her head, blew out smoke.

'Yeah, I did some restoration work in a chapel in Assisi.'

She was class, this girl.

'Not much of that kinda work around here, is there?' I said.

She smiled. Upstairs, Angela squealed. I felt like a total clod.

'No, they just knock down the old buildings, don't they, and put up new town halls and county courts.' she said.

'Right enough,' I said.

'And what do you do?'

'A bit of this, a bit of that. Between jobs like . . .'

4

Here I go, I thought. Make the fucking play. This has worked before. But never with a woman as gorgeous as this.

'. . . but I'm writing this book on Merthyr's heroes.'

I could see the look in her eyes, almost hear her think, Ah, a man of culture in these benighted parts.

That's what I hoped, like.

'Like Dic Penderyn?' she asked. 'Keir Hardie?'

They always ask that. Upstairs, Macky bellowed and the banging got faster.

'Fuck, no,' I said. 'The real characters, you know what I mean? This town is full of them. Clowns and idiot savants. Skinheads and greasers. Where else could you find world-class shepherds and champion ratters? Tell my own story but step out the way when they tell theirs. That's my plan.'

Another scream and roar and the banging upstairs suddenly stopped.

'So, you're a bit of a folklorist,' she said.

'Aye, pub poet, like,' I said.

'Poet, too?'

'Yeah,' I said. 'I'll write a poem about you.'

'You will?'

She beamed. They all do. It's fantastic. I mean, everyone and their uncle wants to be immortalised in verse, don't they? Everything seemed to be perfect all of a sudden. In the silence that was like a bubble all around us while somebody changed the record on the turntable.

'Yeah,' I said. 'I'll write something nice.'

'I'd like that,' she said.

'I think you're really beautiful,' I said.

5

At that point, you are either well in, or they wake up and think that you're a total prat, or something goes terribly awry.

'You're so sweet,' she said. And then, 'Do you dance?'

Fuck. I panicked – my leg, the brace, all that complication, but she was pulling my hand and backing into the crowd with me in tow. Some great reggae started on the sound system – U Roy or I Roy – but I felt like a wooden horse on a roundabout as I undulated around my callipered leg. She didn't seem to mind. Maybe she felt safe with me among the wild men. Sensitive soul, poet and that. Fucking great. I mean. I couldn't believe this, bad leg and all, dancing with Maria Grazia. This dark-eyed Italian girl. Sometimes the stars just fucking line up and there you are. No explaining it. Then there was the surprise of her touch on my hand, my shoulder, my face, this way that she looked into my eyes. I mean. She had to be on drugs.

'I've always liked you,' I said.

'Chemistry,' she said.

Amphetamine, I thought. I could have died and gone to heaven. Then the scent of her. She opened her mouth when she kissed me. Lips soft. Wet. The smoky breath. I already *was* in heaven. She definitely was out of her tree on something. My hand was on her ribs. On her breast. She pulled me towards the corridor through the press of bodies.

Oh my God, I thought, just like that, she wants to fuck me in the kitchen.

'Listen. I've got to leave, OK?' she said.

6

The sails sagged, flump. As they would, wouldn't they?

'Oh. Yeah. Right,' I said.

'Really, I have.'

I nodded. Aye. Too good to be true, like. Of course.

'No, really, listen,' she said. 'My auntie is supposed to come and have a meal at my parents' place. But then they all have to drive up to London tonight, cos they've got a six o'clock flight in the morning. I want you to phone me about half past nine.'

Then she put a piece of paper with her number in my hand. I must have looked stunned.

'Don't worry,' she said.

She kissed me. A peck on the lips and then she disappeared down the passage and the front door slammed behind her. Call her at half past nine. She seemed serious. What the fuck? Give it a go, innit? This was fucking brilliant. And well, hey, there was a lot to do between five in the afternoon and half past nine at night. Set myself up, like. Macky's celebration and that. And that? Not only that. Gerry Black, Big Morgan's brother, was due home on leave from Northern Ireland. ETA: 6.45 p.m. He was rushing from Belfast to Cardiff on the plane. Then up the valley on the train for the big celebration. We'd be lucky if this fucking outing ended before Easter Monday. And here we were, only Good Friday. Gerry was supposed to meet us at the closest pub to the station: the Railway Inn. But, I thought, no matter what happens with Macky and Morgan and Gerry, I am not going to miss out on Maria Grazia. On that I was determined. I mean, trust Macky's timing, to get out of jail on the night when I might score with Maria fucking Grazia. Then I thought, Can't complain, son. Not really. Part of the universal plan, like. If Macky hadn't come out of jail, there would have been no party. No party, no Maria Grazia. Like that. But so much could still go wrong. I'd have to pace myself with the booze and that. Couldn't have Percy letting the side down if I did get lucky. I tucked the paper inside my jacket pocket. Now, I was on a fucking total high. I went back into the front room, I had almost wormed my way through the bodies to the drinks table when Macky's voice bellowed out.

'Hey, Spazzy. How are you, son? Let's go over the Welly for a couple of pints of rough.'

Spazzy. That was what Macky had named me. Everybody has a special name, like, with Macky. Terms of endearment and that. He was back. Thoughts of Maria Grazia faded as Macky loomed into vision. He stood framed in the doorway of that minuscule and massively crowded front room, a veritable giant beside his beneficent blonde waif, though he was, truth to tell, only five foot seven. He was glowing after the sex but his flung-back shoulders and wide-legged stance was all coiled violence. It was fucking great to see him. His face had sort of a boyish bone structure, sharp cheekbones and a pointed chin, not much of a beard and the curly brown hair was still prison cut, short on the sides, and tousled on top. Broken and missing teeth – the result of hundreds of bloody fist fights – showed between his lips that were pulled back in the closest he ever got to a grin. He had a little blue spot tattooed below his left eye, just to make you uncomfortable when you looked at him. His collar was open and his neck was tacked with a set of new and tatty prison tattoos, unreadable stick runes shadowed under his bunched and battered, brown leather jacket. I knew we were going to get hammered if I didn't watch out. He was like one of them old Irish heroes, a man born out of his time, made for rape and drunken pillage, bloody combat and burning villages. Where in centuries gone by he might have ridden across the wilds of Ulster and Connaught, now he was penned within the narrow streets of Merthyr, only marginally less of a prison for him than the grey walls of Swansea Jail. I loved to be around him. You never knew what was going to happen, but it was always a blast. An extreme blast. You just had to watch out that you didn't get caught up in the craziest of his stunts. To join him in a night's celebration could only mean trouble. I had a brief moment's hesitation when I thought of Maria Grazia's smoky kisses but then, how could I refuse? Macky was my mate. He had just got out of jail.

'The Welly? Aye, I'm game,' I called back.

Angela Griffiths looked up at Macky, her large green eyes heavily rimmed with mascara, already filled with the liquid anticipation of impending disappointment. It was highly unlikely he would want to take her to the Welly and she must have known that. It was rare for a woman to be seen there in those days. There was still sawdust on the floor and the clientele was mostly made up of ancient alcoholics, toothless soothsayers, their powers now sapped by venomous fermented brews. The dangerous element was made of the males of gypsy stock who were – like all nomads – fiercely territorial.

9

Macky turned to his girl goddess.

'I'll see you later, love.'

Then he called across the room to Melly.

'Bring this lovely young girl with you down the Rails, Mel. We'll meet you there at nine o'clock.'

The darling Angela Griffiths gave a wan and tragic smile, waved to him. Big Morgan detached himself from Melly's embrace. Morgan had a valleys-wide reputation himself. He was six foot two, broad at the shoulder, narrow at the hip, you know the song, and his hard, angled face was softened by a semicircular scar that curved over his forehead, a semicircle, eyebrow to eyebrow, where someone had glassed him. He was proud of that. He pulled his long hair back behind his ears so it was easier to see. The three of us came out of the terraced house and turned right to get to the high street, two fighters and their crippled scribe.

'Fucking hell, Spaz,' Macky said. 'I haven't had a shag like that for years.'

I haven't either, I thought. I had the jitters. Maria Grazia, would it all work out?

'Not the same in the nick, is it?' Morgan said.

I wasn't sure what that meant. I didn't want to know what they got up to in there. I have never been inside. Lucky or sly enough never to be caught. Or was it cowardice? Leg or no leg, I always managed to slip away from major trouble like a fucking greased eel. Prison is one culture that I never felt the need to participate in first hand. It was bad enough out here. Doing time must be like disappearing down a black hole because whenever anyone came out, it seemed as if it was only last week you'd been with them in the pub. They never bothered to talk about it.

We came out of the narrow lane and on to the high street. I shouted for a taxi and a coal-black Viva pulled up. I told the driver to take us to the first of our battlegrounds. In no time at all we were at the Welly and as the Viva pulled away I saw that it had a rather unfortunate number plate: AHB 666K. Call me fucking Ishmael.

2

Behind the emaciated barmaid, the mirror was grimy, and shot through with rusty veins. Bottles of spirits, dusty and largely untouched, stood reflected in the murky depths, awaiting the day when a too-flush drinker would stray away from rough cider. That time only came about after a lucky bet on a sharp pony – a rare enough event in most parts – or some sudden windfall, some unforeseen act of God that would leave your pockets full for five minutes. The wood of the bar was scuffed and scarred – almost as much as the regulars' faces, these ragged men who stared into the pools of their drinks, their yellow-brown fingers rolling fags from Gutter Virginia – tobacco salvaged from the choice butts they had found lying in the street. The old boys shrouded themselves in smoke, their stained overcoats hanging greasy upon them.

I picked up our pints and swung towards the table. I used the brace on my leg like a pivot to manoeuvre through the splayed legs and lurching customers. The sole of my good foot slid and twisted nimbly on the sawdust that was scattered over the floor to catch the slops from the pint pots. Rough cider. It was all a matter of pacing. Had to be careful. We had time enough for two pints in here before we were to meet Morgan's brother in the Railway Inn. Better not drink any more than that or I'd be in serious trouble if I ever got to Maria Grazia's house.

Macky and Morgan reached for their drinks and clinked their glasses against mine, Macky with that cocky grin and Morgan squinting his already narrow eyes over the rim. They saluted the alkies and the barmaid and then they saluted three gypsies who were gathered together in the far corner minding their own business. Unfortunately, it seemed as if Morgan and Macky had already had some kind of prior acquaintance with them: one Romany, and two Irish tinkers, all weatherbeaten.

Let me tell you now, to get you orientated. There was a gypsy camp up on Collier's Row, and the Welly was the closest pub. The gyppos would come down to drink in ones or twos, or sometimes scads of them. Especially after they'd managed a good antique deal, or been to a horse fair and traded a bunch of old nags for a small fortune. To be fair to them, they did have some good horses now and then. Gypsies stood out among the regulars. They looked healthy compared to the red-raw alcoholic faces of the old boys – those poor drunks, shot to hell at sixty after a life on the cider and in prison and picking seasonal crops. As for gyppos, I never had anything against them really. They were all right. They generally kept themselves to themselves. I liked the way they dressed in battered trilbies and dark bandannas, waistcoats and scuffed paddock boots. They were mysterious, like. All that stuff about them being fortune tellers, I loved that. You never could tell if it was real with them, or if they were nothing but charlatans and thieves. I liked the look of their women too. So did Macky and Morgan. Dangerous business.

After the next pint, Macky made an announcement.

'I'm gonna do a fucking headstand, boys,' he said.

'For fuck's sake,' Morgan said.

Macky made a grab for a particularly rickety chair. He was known for his acrobatics but he was not that good at headstands. They're not easy at the best of times; but with his red eyes and a belly full of cider, he wasn't in any shape to be doing a balancing act. I could tell that the gypsies in the corner didn't think so either. They looked worried as Macky stripped off his shirt.

'Macky, what the fuck are 'ou doin'?' drawled Morgan.

'I wouldn't wunt to be encumbered now, would I?' he said with a certain irritation.

Macky flexed his wiry muscles. His tatty prison tattoos were run through with thick blue veins as he gripped the chair. He had 'Mild' over one nipple, 'Bitter' over the other, and the four suits were arranged between. AFL and an arrow pointed down below his navel.

(I asked him once what it meant. 'All For Liza,' he said. 'Is that a steady woman of yours?' I asked him, though I had never known him to have one. 'Fuck, no!' he answered. 'I broke up with that one as soon as I got outta jail – that must have been the first time I was in.')

13

The calligraphy tacked on to his very real muscles wasn't exactly refined. It's hard to do good lettering with a sewing needle and boot polish, even if you're passing a lot of time in Her Majesty's holiday camp for hard cases.

'Well, go on then, Mack, if 'ou going to,' complained Morgan, and drew on his baggy roll-up. 'What's wrong with 'ou?'

'Hey, I've got to build up to it, 'av'n I?' Macky said.

The gypsies sipped at their cider. They tensed as Macky placed the chair. I was happy enough myself, swallowing the odd mouthful of brew. I watched the reaction of the barmaid, the only woman in the pub. She looked scared. You can't blame her, like.

Macky placed his head on the seat of the chair and gripped its wooden rim. He took the strain and swung his hips upwards.

Feet pointing to the ceiling, he remained poised on that chair for what seemed an eternity – though in fact it lasted only seconds. His legs began to sway.

'Good man, Mack!' I called out, surprised at the sound of my own voice. The barmaid gave him a nervous warning, 'Be careful now, Macky!' and as we all stood stupefied, the chair began to buckle and crack. Macky's back arched. He launched himself in a frantic backflip, a wild attempt to land on his feet.

Glass shattered, cider splattered in a spray and rushing wave over floor and table as Macky's body crashed down among the three gypsies. They dived for cover. There was bloodstained cider everywhere. The barmaid screamed. Morgan yowled in appreciation. The gypsies got up off the floor and all the time gave Macky the cvil eye.

Macky blasphemed and cursed while he thrashed around in front of them. He tried to stand up, to get out of the debris of broken glass and the splintered table. I know he would have done the courteous thing given the chance. He would have stood up, brushed the glass shards off his tattoos, wiped away the blood running in thin rivulets down his bare back and bought the gypsies pints to replace the ones he had knocked over. But you can't talk to gypsies, see. They think you've done it deliberately to wrong 'em. The three of 'em jumped forward and before Macky could regain his balance, fists exploded around his head.

Gypsies are good fighters. But Morgan and Macky were in a class of their own. I don't know how many blows landed on Macky's head and body before Morgan had flown across the room and laid a backhand bottle across the bridge of the Romany's nose. The crack made the cider churn in my stomach. There was a timeless moment before the blood gushed and the gyppo went down. Macky had recovered his poise. He grabbed the throats of the two tinkers in the gaffs of his fingers. He dropped his thick-boned forehead full into the toughest-looking boy's face while the other he pushed off balance. A table went over. All the alkie dole boys gurgled incoherent protests, bewildered as to whether to protect their cider pots or run for cover.

I hate violence. But I had discovered that it often broke out around Macky and Morgan. They never seemed to mind that I didn't join in, encumbered as I was by the brace on my leg. I think they liked to have

15

me around as witness to their actions. I provided some means of objective verification for them, when they would inevitably embellish their exploits at a future date. They were an endless source of stories.

I pulled myself over the bar to escape the fray, hoping the barmaid wouldn't complain. She didn't seem that interested, to tell the truth. She had other things on her mind. Morgan repeatedly slammed a chair on the head of the last staggering gypsy. The tinker just wouldn't go down.

That had to be the end of visiting the Welly for a bit. It was certainly time to make ourselves scarce. There would be police involved. Questions asked. All that.

Morgan and Macky grabbed their jackets; Macky, his shirt too. I ducked under the wooden flap of the bar and struggled after them towards the door.

It was bad. I hadn't even joined in, but I had been drinking with Morgan and Macky. Gypsies have large families, and word gets around Merthyr pretty fast. It was a hell of a way to start a weekend. And it did go through my mind: once you've crossed a gypsy, they could be enemies for life.

3

The doors of the Welly crashed open as Morgan and Macky burst into the street. I was close behind them but – as I spun to my right – I collided with a bloke who wanted to get into the pub. We hit the ground in a tangle of arms and legs, just like a Charlie Chaplin movie.

'Jesus Christ!' he gasped.

'Sorry, butty,' I said, and struggled to my feet. I limped off after Macky and Morgan. They were sprinting down the street.

The bloke on the ground shouted, 'Oi, oi,' and then there was silence when he realised who I was. I knew we were in for a bad night with the gyppos and that, but this had really put the mockers on everything. A fucking bad omen. It was Steven Bunyan. I hadn't seen him for about fifteen years but we both knew each other. We both pretended we didn't.

'It's OK. Forget it.' I heard his voice behind me. I glanced back. Bunyan was on his feet again. He pushed into the pub.

I ran as best I could over Jackson's Bridge. My brain crawled with images of Bunyan, his ugly face, memories of his hands on my hair, the smell of his breath. I didn't want to think about it. It had been a long time ago and it just compounded the confusion of cops and gypsies. I tried to keep my mind on what was happening. Morgan and Macky were close to the Kirkhouse. There was an alley. It would get us away. Off the road. Down by the stinking river where no cop car could pass. It looked so far to that lane. About eight street lights down the road. It was like a fucking nightmare. I ran but I felt like I was getting nowhere. My lungs were on fire. Like running through hot treacle.

You've got to stick together, right? That's what I thought.

I didn't want to think about Bunyan.

This brace is fucking killing me.

The joint dug into my knee on each swivel.

What is wrong with them? I am a fucking witness!

Macky and Morgan were leaving me behind.

And Bunyan's in the Welly. He better not say a fucking thing.

Four more street lights to go. Up in front, my so-called mates made the alleyway and disappeared. No flashing lights yet.

He wouldn't fucking dare.

I forced myself after Macky and Morgan and turned into the lane. I stopped to catch my breath. Gulped some air. I had to go on. Slowly. The alley was pitch black; and silent except for the sound of my one boot – and then the stirrup of the brace on packed dirt. My fingers brushed the brick of the Kirkhouse on my right, on my left the rough stone wall of the Skin Yard. The smell of ancient stockpiled carcasses still lingered in the air. It clung to the walls though the tannery had been closed for years. When I was a kid, we used to go there to get maggots – bait for fishing. We'd come out with a jar of fat larvae, white bodies that would squirm on a barbed hook. I never caught many fish.

I edged forward down the alley, hands out in front now. Blind as a bat as well as crippled. Then the pictures invaded my head, or maybe they appeared in the darkness. Like real. Of Bunyan. I have a frightening capacity for seeing things that aren't there. I can lie in a dark room on my own and it'll be like watching telly, especially on acid or opium. But I didn't need the drugs, like, most of the time. And now, in the blackness of the alley, I couldn't stop it. I didn't want to think about him. I really didn't. But all these pictures came flooding in and I replayed the whole story, sometimes in fragments, in those dark and blind minutes, just like my life flashing before my eyes as if I was about to die. I could see Bunyan's sister Gwyneth. She was my age. Seven. I loved that girl. Gwyneth had this big crush on Elvis, which was great. She had all his records. Even the LPs. And I'd loved Elvis ever since *Jailhouse Rock*. Even when I was four, I used to stand on top of my granny's old valve-powered radio and sing it out, a plastic guitar slung over my shoulder. Me and Gwyneth were listening to 'Hound Dog' on her Dansette. Her brother showed up. He had this great quiff in his hair, just like Elvis, and he was in senior school. I didn't know why but Steven Bunyan seemed to be really interested in me. A little kid. Seven. And him just about a grown-up. In senior school. Then the next day, when Gwyneth and their parents were out, he invited me over his house.

'Let's listen to the King,' he said.

That's great, I thought. He wants to be mates with *me*.

He turned on the Dansette and got a stack of records: 'Return to Sender', 'King Creole', 'Teddy Bear'. He put them on. I asked him, 'Do you go to dances, Steve?'

I thought of the Palace Ballroom. It was legendary. You could see the town's Teds outside in perfect drapes, big bouncers on the doors, girls in pony tails. I wished that I knew what went on inside.

Bunyan looked at me funny and said, 'Yeah,' but I wasn't convinced that he was telling the truth. Then he said, 'Hey, we can dance, I'll show you.' He got up and jerked around to the beat, and then said, 'You try.'

I tried to copy him, but I think I made a better job of dancing than he did, brace or no brace.

'Love Me Tender' came on the Dansette, which I never really liked, because it was slow, and a bit sloppy.

'Hey, Davey,' says Bunyan, 'do you know how to smooch?'

I sort of limped around a bit and said, 'Naw.'

'Well, you have to know how to smooch, if you want to do things to girls.'

I perked up. My brother was always talking about sneaking in to X films. He said they were dirty. At that time, X rating meant any film you had to be sixteen to see. They were usually Hammer horror films, though sometimes they'd be called *Sodom and Gomorrah* or *Splendor in the Grass*. These ones, I knew, were about doing things to girls. So, I wanted to know what Steven had in mind.

'Come on,' he said, 'I'll show you how to smooch.'

So he held me close and moved from side to side. He slid his hands on my back.

'You have to do this to the girl,' he said.

I didn't know what to say any more. If felt nice, but I was scared too. The song finished and he let me go. I wondered why he was so willing to teach me all this about girls.

'Come upstairs,' he said, 'so nobody can see us through the window, and I'll show you some more.'

'OK,' I said, and followed him through the door and up the narrow stairs to his bedroom. I couldn't believe what he had on the wall. There were all these photos of naked women. I remember one of this woman leaning over a snooker table, her tits brushing the baize. I still get a hard-on when I think of that picture.

'Your mam and dad let you put these pictures up?' I said.

Steven looked at me. 'Yeah, they did.'

I thought it was because they were Protestants.

He started in on it then.

'First, I'll show you how to kiss a girl.'

It felt nice. He kissed me on the mouth, and I could feel his tongue sort of poking through his lips. I remember he smelled like my mother's perfume.

'Then you have to feel them, like this. Feeling is pretty dirty too.'

He slid his hands over my back and chest.

'How do you feel?' he said.

It was a bit strange, but I thought I was supposed to be the girl so I said, 'Just like a girl.'

'You do?' he said, as if his ship just came in.

'Yes,' I said.

So he says, 'OK, you be the girl.'

I didn't mind that I was supposed to be the girl, given that the girl was the one to have things done to her that I didn't know how to do. He kissed me again.

Then he said, 'OK. Now we take our clothes off. That's really dirty.'

I said, 'OK, let's try it.' So we took our clothes off, and lay down on the bed. He had these dark brown nipples and hair under his arms and more down by his prick. That looked seriously grown-up.

'Right,' Steven said, 'I'm going to tell you a few things. When you're with a girl, there's kissing and feeling. Then there's bumming and shagging.'

21

'What's that?' I asked,

Steven seemed pretty confident now. 'Well, bumming is when you put your prick up her bum. Shagging is when you put it up her hole in front.'

Well, it was obvious we couldn't do that no matter how well I pretended, and I didn't want anything up my bum. I didn't mind that he kissed and felt me but I didn't see what else we could do.

It got to the time when I had to go home for my tea, and Steven said, 'Come again tomorrow.'

I said, 'OK, I will.'

He said, 'Just think, most people don't learn this stuff until they're a lot older and you're finding it out at seven.'

Right. I couldn't wait to tell my friends in school. They were really surprised by how much I knew. I didn't tell them how I knew, of course, but I became the expert on what to do to girls.

I kept going to Steven's lessons all that summer. We'd kiss and feel and he told me about wanking yourself off, and I told everybody in school. I had quite a reputation, cripple or not. I knew what you did to girls.

It was my uncle put a stop to it all. Unwittingly, of course. He was a social worker. Had this newspaper with an article on homosexuality in adolescents. Big words for a little kid but I was always a good reader.

'What's homosexuality?' I asked him.

'It's like a disease,' he said.

Very fucking enlightened for a social worker.

'What kind?' I said.

'When two boys or two girls start snogging each other. Understand?'

I nodded. I wondered how I had caught it. Playing around drains or something.

'Is it a sin?' I asked him.

'Oh aye,' he said.

'Is it a mortal sin?'

'Definitely.'

I could go to Hell for this, I thought. The only way out was to tell it in confession. And there was still three months to go before my first confession. I had only just begun the instructions about it in school.

I stopped going to Bunyan's after that. Avoided him like the fucking plague. But it was worse later. One night, he caught me in the street.

'Where you been?' he said.

'I can't come over any more,' I said.

'Why not?' he said.

'I just can't, that's all.'

I couldn't explain. I was seven, It was all too fucking confusing. He beat the shit out of me then and told me I'd get more if I told anybody what we'd done. I was scared of him. And then when I was a bit older, I found out that what Bunyan had taught me had nothing to do with girls at all and if my mates found out about what happened, it would be a total nightmare. Fucking Bunyan. I hadn't seen him for years. What a cunt! I wanted to kill him. Knife him, or glass him, or gouge out one of his eyes. I reckoned I was big enough to do it now. But right this second I had to get away. Out of this fucking darkness.

I got to the end of the alley where there was slightly

more light. Behind the buildings, low trees hung their tangled branches over the slope to the river. It was going to be a bitch to get through there with my leg. Now I could hear the water as it shouldered its slimy brown way down the culvert.

I had Macky and Morgan to think about. Why was I hobbling after these two bastards? I had to get out of there. Didn't want the cops to ask me any questions. I mean, I owed it to them as mates, right? Macky anyway. He'd always looked out for me. He said once that he thought I brought him luck. Like a fucking mascot. A bit embarrassing, like. But he was a good mate. You see, in this town, there's always someone who hates you. If I shoot my mouth off, or some bozo gives me a hard time about the brace, or tries to provoke me into a fight, it can get nasty. Macky has got me out of many a scrape. He leans over and whispers psychotic sweet nothings into the other bloke's ear. The guy turns pale, leaves. I wondered if I could work Steven Bunyan into a spot like that. But get him to start swinging. Macky might enjoy it. I know I would. I had to be careful, though, not to push this cripple thing. No fucking self-pity here, like. I felt like shit all of a sudden.

I wondered how far away they were. Maybe they hadn't stopped till they reached the Railway.

Stick together? I thought. Fuck it. I'll have one brew with Morgan's brother. Then I'll split.

I wondered if I'd keep to the plan. I'd still have a lot of time to kill before half past nine. It would be too fucking boring to go home to my flat. Pub's the best place. But you can't drink on your own.

I pushed into the bushes.

'Spazzy!' It was a hoarse whisper. It was Macky. 'Spazzy, over here.'

I gripped the rotten branches and tried to use them for balance, afraid they would break. The dirt crumbled under my feet and I wrapped my arms around a barky trunk to keep from falling.

'Spazzy?'

'Aye, it's me, boys,' I said. 'I'm coming down.'

Gypsies, coppers, Bunyan. And I was supposed to call this gorgeous girl at half past nine. What a fucking night.

Chapter 2

1

Far be it from me to distract attention from the predicament of Macky, Morgan and, of course, myself, but a word is necessary here about certain events that were taking place simultaneously in other parts of town. Events, I assure you, that set in motion the flow of those karmic forces that were to whirl together in Merthyr High Street and explode into mayhem at about twenty minutes before midnight. Each incident on that fateful night had overt or occult influence on what was to follow and I intend to record them all. Or at least, as many as I know.

If you were to float directly south down the river from where we three squatted, you would see the River Taff make its fetid way past the fire station and then slide over the concrete weir where it churns white water. And from there, if you turned inland, crossed the wide bypass and headed east towards the shopping centre for about one hundred yards, you would find yourself at the great concrete and glass redoubt of the Merthyr police station where PC Robert Phillips, at that moment, was backing his panda car out of the parking space in the underground garage. (Ah, PC Phillips, I knew him well. He had been in the same class as me in secondary school and not a *bad* bloke. Over a few pints in the Gurnos Tavern one night, he was willing, even eager, to spill his version of the events in which he had a hand. To give the police side of events. Have I betrayed his trust by telling his story in the fashion which follows? Do I give a fuck? Well, you be the judge.)

Before the eyes of PC Phillips, the lights on the radio blinked. The speaker bleeped to let him know that he could receive loud and clear. An occasional phrase crackled across from the dispatcher, a faceless woman whom he knew only as existing in a room full of knobs and switches and electronic circuits. She sat in that part of the station which he had seen only once. There was too much which he had seen only once. The unfamiliarity of those new surroundings irked him because he was only recently out of police cadet school. He had joined up late to make a new career for himself after six years working at the Hoover factory on the assembly line. He had been laid off in a recent round of redundancies. When he had been in the training school in Bridgend, his instructors had taught him to be hard, arrogant, full of confidence; but his first few days at his new job in the real world had caused his carefully sculpted mask to crack.

There were a fair number of coppers in the station who had been around for a long time and they didn't look at him with much respect. Why should they? He was a new boy. And they made him feel that he had to prove himself. That bothered him, of course. Still, PC Phillips was in the panda car alone. His experienced partner for the night's patrol was waiting for him in a small office in the middle of the town's biggest housing estate, the Gurnos. The desk sergeant had told him to take a panda to get there. He could feel good about that at least. Out on his own. In charge of a car. He flicked on the lights as he drove towards the exit. Most first-time coppers weren't allowed out of the sight of a more experienced partner for months, let alone after only a few days. But the coppers were short-handed tonight. A springtime flu epidemic had made a lot of them call in sick.

Phillips came out of the tunnel of the police station's garage and pulled on to the narrow high street. He drove up past the Conservative Club and the Tankard and the Castle Cinema and the old town hall, massive and Gothic and all red brick. There weren't many private cars around, just the usual lines of taxis manned by those who had recently left the unemployment lines. He knew that a few of them were real hard cases, all tattoos and earrings. They would make mincemeat of him in a fight. But Phillips moved easily through the gears, trying to draw comfort from his uniform. The pavements were populated by groups of schoolkids migrating from pub to pub. He would be on raids soon enough, picking up under-age drinkers of which many a pub was full. Of course, he had been drinking himself when he had been under-age but he would not let that stand in his way. He understood that it was just a game. He was on one side of the line and they were on the other. Their job was to dodge him. And his was to catch them. Nothing much to it really. That's how coppers have to think, innit?

Heads turned as his car approached. Merthyr cops had the reputation of picking people up at night and giving them a good going over if they didn't show the required respect, which hardly anyone would, would they, them being coppers and all? Coppers could rely on strength in numbers. And the support of the courts. The ultimate revenge. Just ahead of Phillips, a group of skinheads was jostling on the pavement. Instinctively, he changed down. The radio bleeped and the dispatcher squawked, 'Call from the Brecon Road. There's been a disturbance at the Lord Wellington. Ambulances are on the way. Are you in the area, Alpha Foxtrot?'

Alpha Foxtrot squawked back as Phillips hit the brakes with a squeal and swerved to avoid a skinhead who had staggered into the road, propelled by a shoulder charge of a brawny mate of his. Phillips cursed as Alpha Foxtrot's voice grated, 'Turning into Brecon Road, off Swansea Road, approaching the scene of the disturbance.'

I was not far from the Welly, still squatting by the river. Phillips was at the top of the high street heading for the Gurnos Estate. Later in the night we would be in the same time and space.

There was a loud beep from the radio. Phillips strayed across the centre line of the road. A car swerved and blasted its horn at him. He jerked the wheel straight again. He turned up the hill. The Avenue hemmed him in with long parallel lines of tall terraced houses. His was the only car, and no pedestrians about either. It was late in the evening, that time of day when people were usually at home or in the High Street and not in any space between. Phillips turned his attention to the road ahead. He wondered what his partner would be like: an ordinary PC like himself but a few years older perhaps? Or maybe some more experienced officer, even a sergeant? He hoped that the older man wouldn't give him a hard time.

The first houses of the Gurnos Estate slipped into place around the panda. He changed down into third as the car laboured up the Gurnos Road. Bad kids up here. He would know a few of them, of course. He lived on the Gurnos himself. Even the young ones had reputations by now: juvenile courts, probation, borstal. Some of the girls he knew were worse than the boys: stabbings with sharpened tail combs, breaking and entering, slashing rivals in romance with carpet knives. Believe me, it's all documented. But Phillips had been brought up better than that. His father would have killed him if he had ever broken into anyone's house and been caught. His father quite naturally filled him with a mixture of fear and affection. Oh yes, the old man had been so proud when Phillips had marched in the passing-out parade, hadn't he? You can imagine how his dad had looked, up there in the stands: grey hair cropped close to his head, his barrel-shaped body straining against the three-piece suit, the tie nearly strangling him. But when Phillips passed by, his habitually taciturn father had yelled like a football fan and jerked an elbow into his wife's ribs, close to knocking her huge handbag from her grip as she clutched it ferociously in two hands. Phillips had taken a few beatings from his father, as had his mother, but he thought of him as a fair man, one who had given this new copper a good set of values. The panda car coasted around the roundabout and Phillips put his foot on the accelerator for the last small hill up to the shopping precinct, night–time stomping ground of the Shop Boys, those darling little skinheads who were to play a major part in the night's violent doings.

2

The sparse grass of the attempted lawn spread out to clutch at old papers and cigarette packets, butts, dead cans and discarded newspapers. The paving-stone walkways were largely ignored, scuffed brown earth spread out all around them. The bus shelter had been wrecked. Likewise the telephone booth, the phone long since ripped out and the solid metal box that had once contained the complex equipment for con-nections and monetary collections was perennially idle, useless and empty, of course. The damp torn pages of the directories littered the floor ankle-deep. The cubicle stank of piss. In the darkness, turned orange by the street lights, hard voices echoed around the low buildings of the shops and the single high-rise tower that squatted behind them. Voices, coarse and adolescent, in thick Welsh accents that you could cut with a knife, if they didn't cut you first. The cold March night had frozen the concrete slabs of the backless benches. The big-boned boys numbed their buttocks sitting on them and they leaned forward to spit liquid streams of phenomenal volume that had gathered in their ravaged cheeks. They pulled on cigarettes, making the tips glow where the shadows fell.

From a distance it would be difficult to distinguish the Firm's members one from the other, dressed as they were in jeans and windcheaters, and with uniformly shaven heads. Those standing moved like amoeba, the gang gradually expanding to split into smaller groups that absorbed yet more newcomers – those who had appeared from the far corners of the housing estate. The Shop Boys they called themselves, and that included the girls, in honour of their gathering place. The windows of the minimarkets, the newsagent's, the butcher's and the fruiterers were all boarded up against them in the night. Spray cans had claimed the shutters for a messy gallery of graffiti, scrawled with the names of Lenny, Bugsy, Ianto and Gripper, in the fuzzy letters of each boy's logo, repeated ad infinitum around the three walls that enclosed the square; and the logos of their lesser cohorts were painted one on top of the other.

Clusters of the girls drifted together, their hair cropped close on top with a few straggly feathered strands falling down on to their coat collars. There was no music, no rhythm, not a ghetto blaster between them, just the odd harsh shout that bounced against the high rise and fell back into the blank spaces between the murmured conversations. Were those more innocent days? Who can say? Back then, there was much less sulphate or smack or any of the common pills and powders that fuel modern mayhem. But none of our protagonists needed it anyway. Most were seriously mental, dedicated to the fanatical pursuit of recreational violence, God bless 'em.

And now an intruder was about to enter the field of their undisputed turf. White and pale blue, a panda car pulled up the hill from the roundabout towards them.

'Old Bill!'

And the gathered crowd rose in unity. The skins let out a mocking cheer for the appearance of the police car. A quick and impetuously snatched bit of broken brick flew from the centre of the crowd and bounced noisily off the roof of the panda car which screeched to a halt – and like a pebble thrown in a pool, its ripples were to spread invisibly through time and space, a cause of utter mayhem, at that moment entirely unforeseen.

Gripper, gangling graffiti artist and undisputed leader of the Shop Boys, was ready for action. Cardiff City were playing away the next day, and he had no money to follow them for his weekly adrenalin rush. There in front of him was potential aggro.

'Nearly knocked his little light off!' he yelled.

And the crowd cheered. Oh yes.

The young copper jumped out of the Panda and slammed the door. No doubt he had hoped to hear a metallic echo in silence, but the noise was lost in the cheer at his appearance.

'Which one of you bloody idiots threw that stone?' PC Phillips shrieked, dismayed, I'm sure, to hear his voice crack into high falsetto.

Now, imagine Gripper as he bounced to the front of the crowd on his cushion-soled Doc Martens, the Cherry Reds making his feet feel like they had wings, arms that swung loosely from his shoulders, the night air – touched with a hint of tobacco and exhaust fumes – that rushed cold into his nostrils.

'Take your pick, copper,' Gripper shouted. 'You lot never bloody care which one of us you get.'

'I'll have you, Gripper, just you watch out,' PC Phillips yelled.

The crowd sank slowly into silence. He knew Gripper. That was bad.

'Aye, when you catch me doing something,' Gripper yelled back.

Phillips didn't push it. He couldn't pick one at random. Not even Gripper. Fuming, he got back into the panda and drove on down the street.

'Bloody scared of us, he was,' Gripper boasted.

He punched his fist against a boarded window, just under his spray-painted name. The echo cracked across the square. He ambled across the precinct.

'Good boy, Grip!'

It was Bugsy. Gripper looked up and grinned. He was glad someone appreciated his showdown with the copper. Bugsy was always trying to emulate him. He was a bit ingratiating even, which Gripper thought was a shitty characteristic in anybody. Bugsy was tough enough, though, and Gripper knew he could count on him in a fight. He remembered how they'd stood back to back against the Liverpool fans when Cardiff had played them in the FA Cup: hardest bastards in football, Liverpool fans. Well, it was between them and Manchester United anyway. (Although, fuck me, think about it: Millwall, West Ham, Chelsea.) It was near legendary, that fight on a building site close to Ninian Park Stadium, and it was a lucky location for Gripper and Bugsy, too, because they'd both found big pieces of wood studded with rusty nails; swung them full force to keep the pack of Koppites at bay.

'Smacked 'em round the earhole,' as Gripper always said. 'Nasty, that. A noisy crack and blood everywhere. Knocked the fucking snot out of 'em.'

Gripper sat down next to Bugsy on the granite bench. He leaned forward, his elbows resting on his bony knees.

'I knew that bastard copper in school,' he said. 'He was always in more trouble than I was. Older than me though. I'd give him a run for his money, if it was just me and him down a back alley.'

'Aye,' Bugsy said, 'they're all show when there's a bunch of them, but shit-scared when they're on their own.'

Gripper grinned at Bugsy's boasting.

Then a group of Shop Boy girls walked by, arms folded and chewing gum. They looked across the patchy grass at the two boys on the bench. One of the girls, a fourteen-year-old, was jabbed forward by Linda Evans who was about three years older.

'Go on, ask him,' Linda said.

The thin kid ventured forward. She glanced back at Linda as she walked up to Gripper. Pay attention, now, because this small event had a significant part in the unfolding of larger ones. It's funny, innit, how things all link together to make up the bigger picture? No one piece without the other. Even just a couple of skinheads who fancied a shag.

'Do you wanna go out with Linda?' the thin kid said.

Gripper scratched the back of his shaven head.

'Tell her we'll have a little talk over by the bus stop.'

Gripper winked at Bugsy and walked across to the broken-down shelter that was spray-painted with his own name in five different colours. Linda broke away from the group and walked towards him, her angled face hard as she approached. He'd always had the feeling she fancied him.

'Hiya, Lind. Let's go for a walk, is it?'

Linda nodded, 'All right, Grip,' and they both moved in the same direction, stiff and awkward, about a foot apart.

'Do you want to come to Cardiff with us next week?' Gripper said.

And then he wondered what the hell had made him invite her to be with him on the terraces of the football stadium when a man needed all his wits about him – though he did think that she could probably hold her own.

'Yeah, great!' Linda said. 'Oh, I can't wait. Against Millwall, innit?'

It went through Gripper's mind that Millwall fans were bloody hard and it was easy for a lot of them to come down from London on the InterCity.

'Aye, that's right,' said Gripper. 'National Front boys, a lot of them.'

'Oh, I can't stand that,' said Linda.

'What's that?' Gripper said. 'Millwall fans?'

'National Front!' she said. 'Fucking Fascists, innit?'

'I thought you was a skin,' Gripper said.

'I am, but I hate fascists,' she said.

Gripper felt a bit confused.

'They're all right, mun, National Front boys. Just having a bit of fun. Paki-bashing and that. It's only fucking nignogs, innit?'

'I fuckin' hate the National Front,' she snapped.

In the face of such vehement passion and Gripper's

eagerness to get into Linda's pants, he could only shrug. Fuck it, it wasn't worth arguing about. He flicked away his fag. He watched the red tip arch across the darkness and spatter sparks as it hit the concrete.

'What's so bad about blacks then, Grip?' she said.

She obviously wasn't going to let him just drop it.

'Well, they're taking all our jobs and that, innit?' he said.

'It wasn't the fuckin' blacks closed down the factories around here, was it? It was the fuckin' Conservatives. You've never hardly seen a fuckin' black up here in the valleys, and everyone's on the dole just the same.'

'Look,' he said, 'if it was blacks, Conservatives, coppers or fucking Millwall fans, it's all a load of bollocks anyway. That, and the National Front. Fuck 'em all.'

He hoped that had pleased her. Linda folded her arms as they walked up the footpath. She was still pissed off. But he couldn't have her slipping away over a bunch of fucking Millwall fans or even the National Front.

'Hey, Lind,' Gripper said. 'Let's go up by the garages.'

Linda's face softened. 'All right, Grip, but don't give me none of that Nazi stuff or I'll fucking do you.'

Gripper liked her better every minute. She knew her mind. She hated the National Front, she was a skin, and that was that. He put his arm around her and breathed his nicotine breath over her. She grimaced and poked him in the ribs. They turned in through a gap in the wall and walked into the shadows, boots scraping on the glass splinters of a shattered street lamp.

'You're all right, Grip, I can tell,' she whispered.

(How do I know? She told me *her* side. He told me *his*. Remember what I said at the beginning? You can trust me. I've been into this story back to front. Witnesses. The full hog. All I do is write it down with slight dramatic embellishment.)

She did fancy him though and, by the way his paws were all over her, she knew he felt the same way. Gripper rubbed the back of Linda's head as they kissed in the shadow of a garage doorway. His other hand cupped around her small breast. She held him close. Her fingertips slipped across Gripper's jeans and took the metal tab of his fly. She unzipped him. She stopped Gripper's hands as he pulled up her skirt and hooked his thumbs in her panties. She thought of crabs, she thought of clap, she thought of pregnancy, but most of all she thought of getting Gripper inside her and Gripper was eager to oblige. She slid her panties aside, and Gripper pressed her against the wall. He lifted her small body and awkwardly twisted his own till he could get into her. And he did. They found a jerky rhythm against the wall. She didn't come but Gripper did and they leaned against each other breathing hard in the dark.

'That was nice, Grip,' she said, politely. 'Even if it was quick.'

They pulled their clothes back into place and went out again on to the footpath. They walked down by the health clinic and crossed the car park where the little police station's window glowed in the concrete wall. They laughed together, poked each other in the ribs.

Then Gripper stopped.

Two coppers had come out of the police station's door. One was PC Phillips, but the other was an older man, a sergeant by the look of him, stripes and that. Gripper felt OK. They couldn't grab him for anything, so he kept on walking towards them. Him and Linda had to pass the coppers to get back to the shopping precinct. First, the coppers just watched them, then started to walk towards them. Gripper had a moment of confusion. Suddenly, the coppers came at him at a run.

'Clear off, Lind!' warned Gripper, and he stepped away from her to stand braced against the coppers' attack. They grabbed him by his arms and slammed him against a red Ford Escort.

'Leave him alone!' Linda screamed out.

The sergeant turned his head and hissed back, 'Piss off, little girl. This bastard's coming with us.'

'Go on, Lind,' called Gripper. 'Go back to the others. I can handle it.'

He was pinned against the car door. The sergeant twisted Gripper's arm behind his back and grabbed him by the neck. PC Phillips had Gripper's other arm. They dragged him off the car and pushed him forward, bending him double, then marched him towards the police station. Linda was frantic. She didn't want to leave Gripper. She couldn't fight them. It would land *her* inside too. She knew they didn't have anything on him. She just prayed that they'd only taken him to try and frighten him and then would let him go. Her fists were gripped tight. She spun in place like a gyroscope. She knew she could make everything worse for both of them.

'I'll be by the shops, Grip!' she called out, and he disappeared into the police station.

3

In his little rozzer office, Sergeant Thomas lit a cigarette.

'Well, it's Gripper, is it?' he said. 'The famous skinhead who knows how to write his own name on any wall around town, but probably doesn't know how to write anything else.'

Gripper was sitting in a straight-backed chair, hunched over, looking at the floor.

'And who was that you were with? Some dirty little slut who let you have it behind the shops, I expect.'

'Fuck off,' Gripper said.

Sergeant Thomas's fist crashed against Gripper's ear. His head jerked sideways, his ear stinging and ringing after the blow.

'Don't you talk to me like that, sonny boy.'

The sergeant's face was all screwed up and he spoke through clenched teeth.

'Don't call her a fucking slut,' Gripper said. He shook, tried to keep himself under control.

'PC Phillips tells me you've been throwing stones at police cars.'

Gripper kept silent. The sergeant insisted.

'Come on, Gripper. It's true, isn't it?'

The sergeant had his face an inch from Gripper's. He could smell the policeman's breath. It was disgusting. Gripper would have liked to have butted him.

'I haven't done anything.'

'Haven't done anything! You're always in trouble, Gripper.'

'Come on, Grip,' PC Phillips said like a total wanker. 'It'll go a lot easier on you if you own up now.'

Gripper didn't say a word. PC Phillips leaned against the table in front of him.

'Look, Grip, we'll help you out if you just cooperate with us. You're in a lot of trouble already; so, if you play the game with us, we'll see that the court goes easy on you.'

'I haven't done nuthin,' Gripper said.

Thomas grabbed him by the back of his windcheater collar.

'Sit up when we're talking to you, boy. Have you got that?'

Gripper clenched his teeth. He had to keep his temper under control so that he didn't do or say anything stupid. He was really scared that the sergeant was going to lay into him with a truncheon pretty soon.

'You'd better own up, boy, or I'll make your life bloody hell. Do you understand me?' Thomas was spitting as he spoke.

Gripper said nothing.

'Do you understand me? I want an answer!' the sergeant screamed.

Gripper felt confused. The room started to look out of balance. There it was. The sergeant had his wooden club in his hands. The leather wrist strap looked worn. He was slapping the truncheon against his palm.

'I don't like little toerags thinking they can throw stones at a police car,' he said. He cracked the club down hard on the edge of the desk. PC Phillips looked at Gripper with mock stern concern.

'Make it easy on yourself, Grip,' he said. 'We'll help you out if you make a statement here. That is, if you do it before we take you down to the main station, in town. Down there, you know, there'll be hell to pay.'

Gripper turned pale and cold. He felt as if he needed to shit. They weren't just going to let him go. He thought of saying he'd done it just to get out of there, but he knew he was in for a trip down town anyway.

I'm saying nothing, he thought, and almost to his surprise he said, 'I haven't done a fucking thing. Now, leave me alone.'

Thomas slid the truncheon around Gripper's throat and pulled back as if to throttle him. Gripper choked. The sergeant suddenly let go.

'All right, Gripper, my boy. Let's be taking you down to the station where we can really sort you out. Put the handcuffs on him, Phillips.'

Phillips cuffed him and spun Gripper towards the door. Thomas pushed him into the street. Phillips turned out the lights behind them and locked the little office. They bundled Gripper into one of the pandas. Thomas sat behind the wheel.

'Bring the other car, Phillips,' he said.

'I'll be right behind you,' Phillips said.

The two pandas pulled out of the car park.

4

As they passed the shopping precinct, Linda yelled out: 'They're taking him away. They've got Gripper!'

In one voice, the skinheads in the precinct let out a wordless roar and jeer, and then looked on, powerless, as the panda cars disappeared down the hill.

'We've got to do something,' Linda said.

A gust of wind tumbled balled-up newspapers and empty brown paper bags around her scuffed Doc Martens. Bugsy knew that Gripper would have come up with an idea that would have had them cheering each other on; but Bugsy wasn't sure what it would be. Linda was showing him up. Everyone looked to her.

'Let's go down town and cause a bitta bovva,' Bugsy shouted.

'What bloody good is that going to do?' Linda said.

'You'll see!' Bugsy yelled.

And although he didn't see what use it was going to be to Gripper, he still thought that it would be better than listening to Linda.

Bugsy broke into a loping run across the littered patch of grass, shouting, 'We are the Shop Boys! We are the Shop Boys!'

Anto, Ianto, Gobbles and Shiner joined in the chant. The whole group in the shopping precinct moved after Bugsy. They all joined in the chant. Linda stood disgusted. Annie Pritchard called out: 'Come on, Lind! Let's see what happens,' and she ran after the crowd of skinheads. They headed en masse down the hill towards the roundabout on the first leg of their journey towards town.

Bugsy was out in front and Anto was at his shoulder, little Gobbles and Shiner just behind.

'Oolie oolie, oolie oo! Who the fuckin' hell are you?'

'Shop Boys! Shop Boys! Shop Boys!'

They kept up the chants as they went on. Bugsy felt his blood rise like it did on a Saturday afternoon at Ninian Park when the crowd surged. It felt great to be on the march together down the deserted street. He knew it was up to him to make the Shop Boys buzz down through the Gurnos Estate until they could explode against something in the Friday-night High Street.

'Shop Boys!' crack! – crack! – crack!

'Shop Boys!' crack! – crack! – crack!

The sharp staccato of their yell and clapping echoed down the street.

Bugsy felt the mob swirl around him. He hoped to meet more skinheads down in town, suck them up into his crew and see if they could do some real damage.

'No fucking Gripper here, boys,' he yelled. 'No fucking Gripper here. Just me. Just Bugsy. And we're all going to get him out.'

Out on the pavement was an empty pair of shiny metal rubbish bins. Bugsy flipped one up by its handle and swung it up over his head. He hurled it with all his strength into the middle of the road. It clanged and banged its way down the tarmacked gradient of the hill while Anto grabbed the other bin. He swung around with it like a hammer thrower at the Olympics and launched the dustbin through the air after the other one. The loud clang made the mob howl and they chased after the rebounding bins to kick them on down, all along the Gurnos Road. Bugsy knew he had them going. The Shop Boys were now a single animal and Bugsy was its brain and the charge hammered through his veins. Have you ever felt that? On the terraces at a football match? On the streets when a demonstration gets really fucking charged? Gets violent? It's a fucking buzz, I can tell you.

The skins swarmed down the street. They snapped off side mirrors and radio aerials of the cars parked along it. They yelled and jeered as they saw a couple in the distance hurry off the Gurnos Road in the face of the approaching menace. Bugsy screamed at the top of his lungs. His face was red. He was bug-eyed. He was superman.

Linda watched the mêlée careen down the street; gradually the skins gained distance from her. She stopped to light a cigarette. She felt a wetness drip into her panties. The thin cotton became a little cold and uncomfortable. She needed to see Gripper. Whatever the fuck Bugsy did, she couldn't believe that it was going to set Gripper free. But loath though I am to say it, my friend, that is where she was wrong.

Chapter 3

A match flared. I saw Macky's face in the glow as he cupped his hands around flame and fag. Morgan's head swung momentarily into the light, then disappeared behind a puff of smoke as the match went out.

Two little red glows and the smell of tobacco.

'Any sign of the coppers, Spaz?' It was Morgan's voice.

'Nothing, son.' I said it flat, but I was still tamping that they'd left me behind like that.

'I can't believe it, Spaz. I'm only out ten hours and I can't go and have a quiet drink without some gyppo starting a fucking war.'

That slowed me down. I could see that Macky was right. He was right to run. I didn't have much of a stake in it. But if the coppers pulled Macky and decided to stitch him up on a GBH charge, he could be down again for years.

'We'll sit by here for a minute now an' 'en we'll stroll over the Railway to meet Gerry,' Morgan said.

I wished at that moment that I hadn't given up the foul weed a year ago, as my cohorts squatted and smoked in silence. I brooded on the fickle circumstances that had brought me to know these two hard bastards in the first place. It was something to do while we waited, and would keep my mind off Bunyan. I looked into the darkness, like in the alley, and let pleasant pictures come. Sixteen I was when I met first met Macky and Morgan through my closest friend at the time, a boy called Harry Williams aka Harry Krishna aka Priest. We shall come to know more about the origin of his name later on but at this time we were still in secondary school and had just begun to get interested in the drugs that went along with rock and roll. Harry looked older than me and he didn't attract attention the way I did with the gammy leg. We used to take a train down to Newport and while I waited in a café he would go into a pub on the docks to see if he could score some hash. There was plenty about and he would buy a quarter-ounce off the dockers. We split the dope up into quid deals: five to the quarter.

After a good score, we'd go up to his house of an afternoon and have a few joints. We'd sit on the back step to the garden. His parents were out, of course. After the draw, we'd go into his front room. It always smelled of synthetic fabric. The furniture was all buff plush and fake mahogany. The sofa and two armchairs could swallow you whole in their overpowering upholstered depths. The room was a monument to hard-earned affluence and the limits of the valley's furniture shops. But Harry had a killer stereo system. We cranked up the volume on the amp, faced each other enthroned in armchair spacecraft, and blasted into *Electric Ladyland* or *Wheels of Fire*. Come four o'clock, we'd have to shut down the system because his dad came home from work and we didn't want to face him stoned. There was only one place to go and that was the Queen's Café.

Me and Harry rolled all over the high street. From among the grey normals, we saw Morgan and Macky appear like electric angels from Hell. They were all tattoos and gnarly scars. I knew them by sight, of course. They had big reputations by then. They'd been in and out of borstal and jail loads of times. Harry knew them because he drank in a cider pub called the Olde Expresse, where the landlord didn't care if you were under-age. Morgan and Macky drank there because cider drinking was the cheapest way to get drunk.

'Harry, mun, 'ow are 'ou son?' greeted Morgan. Macky didn't say anything, just opened that grin, with the missing teeth, in a friendly grimace.

'Oright, Morg,' Harry offers. 'What's appnin' then?'

'Just had a few pints down the Rails, mun. Ready for a bit of tea in the Queen's.'

'Do you know Davey, boys?' Harry asked.

'Never seen 'im before,' Morgan said.

'Hiya,' I said, stone-faced.

'Got a bit of blow, is it boys?' remarked Morgan, picking up on the bloodshot eyes and half-open mouths.

'Got a quid deal, if you want it,' said Harry.

'Fuck, aye,' replied Morgan. 'Let's go in by here.'

'Come and have some coffee and a pie, boys. I'm fuckin' starving,' said Macky.

We trooped into the Queen's Café. Macky looked sideways at me as I limped in.

'I'm going to call you Spazzy,' he said, 'because of that thing on your leg.'

I looked for a snappy comeback but it twisted away unformed in an unintelligible Afghani echo of the café sounds. The roar of the milk steamer. The cries of the waitresses. The tables and chairs shone in a golden glow. It sounded like Macky was talking down a tunnel anyway so I didn't care that much. People had been making comments about the brace on my leg for years. The brace was a part of me. It had been attached to everything that had happened in my life since before I could remember. I'd certainly got used to it. He would have to try another tack. We slid behind the yellow Formica table. The waitress was gorgeous. We ordered coffee and steak and kidney pies.

'You got that blow, Harry?' Morgan asked.

Harry slid across the table a piece of 'Ghani black wrapped in silver foil.

'Lend us a quid, Mack,' Morgan said.

Macky palmed the note to Harry.

'Nice bit of shit, that,' Morgan said.

The waitress sauntered back and banged four steamed pies down on the table.

'There 'ou are, boys.' Accent: Welsh Mediterranean. Incongruous, beautiful. She left to get the frothy coffees. I knew she was the daughter of the café owners, Italian as they were. She was a little bit chubby with dark corkscrew hair. I guessed that she was a couple of years older than me.

Harry told me her name later. It was Maria Grazia. Every time I went to the Queen's after that, I hoped that she was going to be the waitress. But I was always too scared to ask her out. She was unreachable.

'You're about the same age as my brother Gerry,

you are, Spaz,' said Morgan. 'He went off a couple of months ago to join the forces. In a very brief period, they've turned him from a scrappy little kid into a fucking killing machine. Fucking amazing, really.'

Morgan obviously had me pegged for a peace freak because I was a friend of Harry.

It was then it dawned on me that I had gone to infants school with this younger brother of his called Gerry. I recognised the resemblance now. I didn't say anything. I felt a bit uneasy. I mean, why would a once-good Catholic boy like Gerry join a commando group whose express purpose was to terrorise Catholics in Northern Ireland? It gave me the creeps. It must have shown.

'You're a very pensive sort of bloke, I'd say, Spaz,' said Morgan. 'You have to be fucking careful thinking like that.'

I wondered what he meant. Could he read my mind? He was fucking getting to me. He was playing the paranoia game. Morgan elaborated. 'In this world, see, Spaz, there's two kinds of people: there's predators, and there's victims. Now I'm a fucking predator, I am, son. What do you think you are?'

Before I could answer, Macky cut in, 'Fuck off, Morgan, you'll frighten the boy, mun.'

Morgan poked at his pie to let the heat out of it. 'I asked you a question.' Macky didn't interrupt again, but I was still distracted by the waitress. I just blurted, 'I don't know what you mean, Morgan. People are just people, innit?'

But it sounded so hollow.

'Fucking people are just people.'

There was contempt in his voice. I was to find out

50

later that Morgan was a philosophical man. He was well read. His world view was directly derived from Conan the Barbarian. He had read all of them in jail, not just Robert E. Howard but all the knock-offs too: L. Sprague De Camp and that.

Macky grabbed his plate and ran thick strands of brown sauce up and down the length of his pie, zig-zagging over the soggy pastry that sagged after being steamed. He lifted a forkful of the blistering stodge and it disappeared into his waiting mouth.

'I could eat anything,' Macky said.

'He's not fuckin' jokin' either,' Morgan said. 'You should have seen him last Saturday. There was me and him tripped out of our fuckin' brains. We'd just scored ten tabs off Foxy, see. Duw, it was the strongest acid I've ever had.'

Well, at least he'd changed the fucking subject. He leaned over the table. Full of enthusiasm now he had a real story to tell.

'Now there was these three gypsy girls in the lounge of the Rails. They must have been bad girls because they had given their men the slip, like. They're flirting a bit with me and Macky. So I thought, Chance for a bit of fun, innit? I crushed up a couple of tabs and dropped 'em in their beers. After about an hour, they didn't really know what was going on except that we had definitely spiked 'em with something. Booze had mellowed the acid coming on, so they're not too freaked, you know.

'So I says, "Well, let's enjoy it, innit? We'll go for a walk up the park." Now, two of them have got the hots for Macky. This fat one called Bridey, and a beautiful skinny one called Clara. The other girl clutches on to me for dear life.'

He turned to Macky. 'What was she called, Mack? Theresa, wasn't it?' Macky shrugged. Morgan continued.

'Anyway, with the old brain in meltdown, the other two are rubbing themselves against Macky. Now, Mr Suave Man wants to impress them. He says, "Hold up a minute, girls." Then he sets off to poke around this drystone wall. He catches six big hairy spiders in the cracks and just to freak the trippers, he pops them into his mouth and starts eating 'em alive.'

Me and Harry looked at each other in disgust.

'So here's Macky with the live spider hors d'oeuvres and the three gypsy girls wailing. The skinny one screams at him, "Macky, the day you eat a dog will be the day you're fuckin' doomed."

'I cracked up laughing, I did. I mean, here he is, eating spiders and she's on about fucking dogs. People say the craziest things on acid, don't they? Anyway, to my surprise, Macky looked like he'd seen a ghost, when she said that.

'"I'll never refuse anything a woman offers me," he says.

'I was fuckin' roaring laughing, it was getting so weird. Nobody was making any sense, like.'

Macky elbowed Morgan in the ribs and picked up the story, waving his fork around for emphasis.

'It was like this, see. Christ, there was a sort of . . .' – he paused – '. . . palpable darkness that gathered in the air above us.' (His mouth rolled the word 'palpable'

52

with obvious enjoyment.) 'I was just waiting for the bats to appear out of it.'

He popped a piece of hot pie into his mouth, and talked as best he could around it.

'She looked like a fuckin' witch. She says, "Do you know what Cyfarthfa means in Welsh?" "No." I says. "The place of the barking dogs." she says.

'Morgan nearly died laughing. What she was saying didn't make much sense, like, but all of a sudden, it scared the shit out of me. I'd frightened myself half to death.'

'Oh aye,' said Morgan. 'There's nonsense, innit? But we were all right after a couple of pints of Vat down the pub. Macky even ended up fuckin' this Clara. I tell you, the fat one didn't like that one bit. And she got all huffy too when I offered to poke her for a consolation prize.'

I knew I had to be on my guard with them, but right then, I liked something about being around Morgan and Macky. It was the sensation of being at ease in the world of evil. Safe. I knew I could learn something from them. I liked the storytelling of their exploits, the pranks, the quick way they snapped into violence and never gave it a second thought. I envied that in them.

We live in a small town. If you share certain interests, especially illegal ones, it's inevitable that you find the same people in the same orbit. If you were into love, peace and the expansion of consciousness, or fucking, fighting and brain derangement, the sources of metaphysical fuel were the same. Market fluctuations demanded mutual respect. Given that we also had the same enemy in the police, it was natural that we stuck together. I found myself with them more and more, especially after Harry went away to college.

Upriver, blue light stabbed the night. We heard the sound of sirens. 'One cop car. One ambulance. No problem, son,' Macky said. We waited in the dark. I reckoned it would take ten minutes for them to load the injured on the wagon. Then we would be safe to go. The cop car had turned its light out. No one would talk in the Welly. Sandra the barmaid was cool. The gyppos would want to settle it all themselves. Fucking Bunyan, man. He better keep his fucking mouth shut. We listened. Everything was still quiet.

It was close to Gerry's ETA but fucking Bunyan was in my head again. What was the connection with Gerry and Bunyan? There *was* one and it was gnawing at the edge of my consciousness. Gerry. Bunyan. Confession. Communion. Confession, my son, confession. That was it. Preparing for confession. And subsequent communion. All those fucking years ago. One of the last times that I ever saw Gerry Black was in infants school. Of course. Now, I had uncovered the very incident that was the cause of Gerry joining the SAS. The Special Air Service specialised in undercover work. They ran plain-clothes death squads in Northern Ireland. Listen to Herr Doktor Spazzimund Freud and see why Mr Gerry Black turned assassin of his own people. And how come Steven Bunyan reared his ugly head into my life precisely now? See how forces unleashed way in the past came to be brought together on this night. Confession, my boy, and Holy Communion. It was all linked up. It's creepy the way this undercover unconscious works.

Back then, when I was seven, I couldn't wait to go to confession because of the Bunyan incident. Gerry Black was in the same class as me in school and as short-arsed as I was at the time, a snaggle-toothed brat with a home-cut basin hairdo. Though how we do change when we enter adulthood, how we do change. Me and him were always in the front of the columns of kids arranged by height – the Corpus Christi procession, the May procession, and then the march to the altar rails for the first communion. We were to be the first to walk down the church aisle to get the first communion wafers laid on our upturned tongues. We were to receive into our mouths the body of God Christ Himself. We would be flooded with Grace, like a divine spatial ambrosia erupting into that entity hidden somewhere inside mind and body and known as the soul. The Divine Bread was the nourishment needed to feed the immortal spark ignited by the breath of God Himself. I had felt so close to Gerry Black. We were to eat the flesh and blood of God and merge with His very being, me and Gerry together. I thought then that must have made us like brothers. (That would make me Morgan's brother too. And Macky was like a brother to him . . . ergo, et cetera . . .)

The reverse side of the coin had been confession. That had scared us. Up until this point in our lives they had considered that we hadn't reached the age of reason and so sin had had little hold on our immortal souls, protected as we had been by baptism. Now our eternal fate was in our own hands. We could sin and pollute our souls so that they would shrivel up to a dried blackened walnut of a thing, fit only for eternal charcoal on the torturing hobs of Hell; or we could cultivate grace and goodness and get a seat up close to the throne of God as He sat in the eternal banqueting halls of Heaven. Of course, I planned to get the seat closest to the Almighty, down by the skirts of Jesus, but I was already sitting in the catechism classroom with a scorched soul courtesy of Steven Bunyan, and revealed unto me by my uncle. Scary as this confession was, I was ready for it. I had to get the Bunyan sin off my soul. So the day before our first communion, me and Gerry sat outside the dark wooden box waiting for the priest to pull the rope on the door and let us in to our first confession. I had to go first. The door swung open. I entered and saw the metal grille and red leather curtain. Inquisitional. There was something disquieting about the set-up. Perverse somehow. Fetishistic, that was it. I could see it all now. The priest began mumbling in Latin. I kneeled down by the grille.

I began. 'Bless me, Father, for I have sinned, this is my first confession.'

I told the presence behind the curtain everything I could remember.

'Against the first commandment . . . Against the second commandment . . .' and on into my shameful sins.

Even the sixth commandment, thou shalt nor com-mit adultery. Adultery meant doing things to girls. Worse, if with boys, as my uncle had said.

'Against the sixth commandment, I have had wrong thoughts and done wrong deeds.'

Not a word from behind the curtain. Silence. I was a seven-year-old kid. I could almost hear the priest think, What the fuck does he know about it?

I had done it. I had confessed the sins with Bunyan without needing to go into detail. And I was going to get absolution.

'Against the seventh commandment, I stole a bit of clay from school. Against the eighth commandment . . .'

I came outside and Gerry went in. I was free. Bunyan, cleared out. Me, full of grace. I started my penance in the pews opposite. After a garbled Our Father and a few more Hail Marys, my soul was ready to receive its divine nourishment. Gerry, second man in, then appeared from the box, winked, thumbs up and joined me in the pew. He began his penance. The blots and stains we had put on our souls had been removed. We went out into the sunshine together. Outside the church we said our Seeyatomorrers, excited. Next day was first communion day. The day when Gerry's fate took the turn that turned him into a Catholic-killer.

My mother got me to the church hall early. Gerry Black hadn't arrived yet. All the boys were dressed in white shirts, white shorts, white socks and white gym shoes. The girls had white veils, white dresses, white socks and white sandals. The mothers fussed and doted in unspoken competition to make their child the prettiest, most perfect and most holy of the budding first communicants. Gerry was the last boy to arrive. There he was, ready to walk down the aisle to the carved marble altar rails. In front of the whole school. The whole parish. He was dressed in white shirt, white plimsolls, white socks, and worsted, woollen, *grey* trousers. Grey and worsted trousers, not white and cotton. They were obviously his very best pair of trousers, but they were *grey*. I saw the horrified look in the maternal eyes. Violet Coughlin's mother glared at Gerry's mother. Mrs Black shuffled nervously among the other mothers who primped and preened their white-clad offspring. She looked at the hostile Mrs Coughlin and said to her: 'Well, they said to have him in white trousers but I only just spent a good bit on these new ones for him for school, so I didn't see why I should lay out again for something he'll only wear once, do you?'

Mrs Coughlin's face clouded. The skin was mottled black and hot red. 'For his first communion, he should be wearing white, that's all.'

Mrs Black blanched, white as my lily-white shorts, exposed under the pinch-faced glares of the other women, all directed at her and her son. I felt sick to the pit of my stomach.

From the reaction of these Catholic grown-ups, I thought that maybe Gerry's mother was one of those 'Catholics-in-name-only' that we were warned about in school. One of those who never went regularly to church. Doomed to an afterlife in Hell. Was this the proof of it? Those tell-tale grey trousers among the lily white? Her own blanched face an admission of guilt. The clique of fussing mothers looked like a flock of predators pecking at an injured bird. Gerry's face twisted in embarrassment and confusion. I put my arm around Gerry's shoulders to make him feel like my brother in Heaven again, but I have to admit I was suspicious of him. And I knew that damage had been done. Not long after, Mrs Black took Gerry out of our Catholic school and sent him to the state one. Fuck me. The proof of the pudding and all that. In name only. I never saw Gerry after that. I wondered if he'd remember me. I was convinced that that first communion experience had had a heavy influence on Gerry's choice of career. There was one sure destination for any squaddie in the British Army at the time he joined, and since: that was the streets of Northern Ireland. Tonight would be another unholy reunion as it had been with Bunyan.

Gerry Black – Catholic-killer. Steven Bunyan – child molester.

Both dark spectres of the papal past had come back into my life on this Good Friday night. I was anxious. I could sense that the boys were uneasy too. If a horde of gypsies came tracking us down, there was likely to be something of a public spectacle. Being an SAS man, Gerry Black wouldn't want to keep a high profile anywhere, even under civilian circumstances. Morgan was not a sentimental man but he had been looking forward to this double celebration: Macky, his best mate, out of jail; and his brother coming home from Northern Ireland. Everything was suddenly in jeopardy. I dare say Gerry would probably be able to handle the situation with maximum efficiency. It might even be something to look forward to.

Macky raised himself from his squat. Upriver, Jackson's Bridge had been silent long enough. Just the odd swish of a taxi going over it.

'All right, boys,' Macky said. 'Time to go to the Rails.'

We climbed up from the river bank towards the waste ground behind the pop factory. It was good to be on the move again. I was curious to meet Gerry Black again. I thought it would be like meeting the Angel of Death himself, the man who would complete this triumvirate of evil: Macky, Morgan and Gerry. I wondered if it would be enough to face the gypsies when they came, as come they certainly would. What other unspeakable horrors did the night hold? We pushed our way through the hanging branches and left the river behind.

Chapter 4

1

Maeve Daunt sat in front of the telly in her own front room in a two-bedroom council house on the Gurnos Road. When she heard the crash of a dustbin outside her window, she instinctively hunched her small body over her knitting. She stopped sucking on her boiled Minto, though her fingers, unstoppable, continued to plain and purl a baby's jumper. On the telly, Val Doonican crooned a sentimental ballad. He was dressed in his white pullover, perched upon his tall stool while Maeve Daunt, my mam as it happens (there now, doubt not the relevance of this little cog and gear), whom I had not seen in six years, felt her blue-rinsed hair prickle on her head.

They're shouting those stupid chants, Maeve thought. Sounds like at least thirty of them.

She resisted the urge to run to the window. A spontaneous prayer fluttered on her lips for herself, for her husband, for my brother Roger, the good one – and for me no doubt, crippled Davey, the family's black sheep. I believe in prayer and the power of prayer. I really do. Doubt it not. And what would a Welsh story be without a mam? Even if it's only just a cameo, like. Have you ever seen a story on BBC Wales, or in the *Western Mail*? There's always a fucking mam. Any Welsh personality shows up in a feature programme and there it is, like, they have to show their fucking mam. So, far be it from me to buck the tradition. I mean, as you know, I am very much into tradition. This whole story is about tradition, myth, blood, how they all shape us and that, drive us to where it's almost as if we have no control over ourselves, forces beyond us, is it not? And the Gurnos Estate is not just full of skinheads and yobs, you know. It is also full of their mams, a fair proportion of whom might very well be decent people. And some not, no doubt. Maybe the estate is not so full of their dads. The dads are probably down the pub, as we shall see. But anyway, no one springs into being out of the thighs of mighty Zeus, as it were. Certainly not me. And this story would not be complete without a taking into consideration the effects of the night's events on one of these mams, and the effect that she might or might not have had upon the shaping of the events, albeit on a somewhat supernatural level. I present the facts. You make the judgement.

As I said, I had not seen her for six long years. But why is this, you may ask? The answer cannot be supplied in a few cold words. Perhaps it may be inferred from the surroundings in which we find her and by the addition of a few small facts of my life before the break-off of diplomatic relations.

See the room.

Maeve's eyes fixed upon the statue of the Virgin Mary that stood among white lilies on the blue-draped table next to the telly. Pride surged. Her fears abated.

She prayed that her family would survive the easily imaginable dangers of even a normal night in Merthyr, let alone this one. There is power in such prayer directed to such an image. I am not being facetious. This statue of the Virgin belonged to the Society of Our Lady of Dalkey. It had been blessed by Father Thomas Murphy, once a shepherd, now a priest, who had seen an apparition in this very form, on the hills above Dalkey while he wandered in the grip of spiritual crisis. Maeve knew his story from a society pamphlet that she had since memorised. Let me quote from it, for I know it. Yea, I know it well.

It was said that as he passed the abandoned tower above the town he was struck down by a blinding flash of light; and as he recovered his senses, he saw the luminescent form of the Blessed Virgin standing with her foot upon the head of a snake.

The shepherd knew that this was no ordinary woman for St Patrick had rid Ireland of all serpent life. The apparition raised her eyes to gaze into the very soul of the doubting shepherd and he was so moved by the supernatural vision that he was filled with holy shame. Such faith overwhelmed him that his hands and feet began to bleed. His shirt was saturated with blood from an oozing lesion that had opened below his breast.

Lilies bloomed on the very spot where the apparition stood, and the little brook that bubbled among the rocks below the tower had been imbued with such miraculous power that it cleansed the faithful of sin. It brought health to the chronically ill with sufficient faith in the apparition of Our Lady of Dalkey.

The Church authorities had been slow to give their official recognition that this had been a genuine apparition. Careful examination always needs to be made of such a claim. The shepherd's display of the stigmata gave credence to his story. The miraculous cures attributed to the stream were certainly undeniable. A small shrine has been built at the place; and the Society of Our Lady of Dalkey has begun to carry out the devotions described to the shepherd by the communications of the marvellous apparition.

It was Mrs Dorothy Quinlan who brought the Society of Our Lady of Dalkey to the Welsh valleys' parishes. She was an ardent Irish woman who had come over the water to serve as house-keeper to a local priest. Yearly pilgrimages set out by bus from the valleys, bound for Dalkey, via Holyhead and Dun Laoghaire. At the Irish ferry port, they take the short train ride to the holy village. There the pilgrims ascend the hill bearing candles and singing hymns of praise to Mary, the Mother of God.

Statues have been made on the instructions of the shepherd turned priest. They depict the Virgin with her foot upon the head of the serpent, Lucifer. Each chapter of the Society is given a statue, and each of its members is instructed to be custodian for a fortnightly period so that the bless-ings of Our Lady of Dalkey can enter the house and bless the families of the Society's members.

I believe in apparitions. And the stigmata. And I believe in whole lot more too. Which has left me at odds with the Church of my forefathers. I believe in ghosts and demons and ancestral spirits and a pantheon of gods and mysterious malevolent and benevolent forces that would fill the universe with infinite multiples of the number of angels who could fit on the head of a pin. Maeve was not of that persuasion. And who am I to criticise her beliefs when mine are so outlandish?

Maeve, in her two-week guardianship of the statue, had never lost an opportunity to show to her friends and visitors the blessed image, touched by the hand of the stigmatised priest. As outside the window passed the drunks, the cursers and the blasphemers, the statue shone forth rays of holy purity. You may have already inferred the general reason why one foul-mouthed and drug-besotted scribe had no place here. This room, this very house, had been hermetically sealed by Maeve to keep that world beyond the window securely at bay while I, even at a young age, wanted to explore, embrace, dissect and immerse myself totally in that raging maelstrom, viz., the experience with Bunyan at the age of seven, which added to the adolescent embrace of atheistic Marxism emphatically proscribed by the declarations of Our Lady of Fatima, and the eruption of Eros and excessive ingestion of hallucinogens, coupled with one Sunday morning's stubborn refusal to set foot any more inside the Catholic church, were all to result in the attempted murder of one Davey Daunt, cripple or not, by his mam, Maeve Daunt, first with a kitchen knife, then with the axe used for cutting sticks for the fire, then with her husband's shotgun, previously used for shooting rabbits, which left a large hole in my bedroom wall. The failure of all these methods, however, did lead to my enforced eviction from the house of my childhood. Ah well. That was then. This is now and I'm well out of it. So let us not dwell on the past. This is solely by way of explanation of why word had not passed between us for six years. An aside, as it were, to our main story.

What, you may ask, is Welsh about this mam with her Virgins and Val Doonicans? Should she not be chapel? And speak Cymraeg? Well, where else does she belong? Born and bred in Merthyr. Father, Irish miner, devout Catholic born in Cork; her mother, Catholic convert, born in Aberdare, native of Merthyr from the age of fourteen, mother to Maeve at eighteen. And Maeve had never been out of Merthyr until she was twenty-four and went on her honeymoon to London. Who defines Welsh? Richard Llewellyn? How green was my fucking valley? Gimme a break. Spend a bit of time in the Gurnos, or on the Ely Estate in Cardiff, or in Tiger Bay. Fuck it, even Shirley Bassey's black.

The brash voices of the skins receded down the street. Maeve heard the muffled clatter of another tossed rubbish barrel, further away. She put down her knitting and got up to risk a peek through the curtains. A young girl stood on the kerb, with what Maeve read as a blank expression on her face. She watched the girl light a cigarette.

'There's a shame that she's so young to be starting such a bad habit.'

The girl began to walk in the direction of town, following the gang that had already disappeared. Something in Maeve wanted to reach out to her.

'Perhaps she would like to have a cup of tea. I could ask her what was wrong.'

Maeve felt the opportunity to talk to the girl, to influence her life, slip away from her. The girl continued down the street. Maeve added the girl to her prayers for the Virgin's intercession. We'll see if her prayers had an answer.

2

A hellish crack of lightning split the black night with blazing white. The ground shook. We ducked under Heaven's concussion. Stunned, we looked at each other in the sudden silence. In the next instant, the deluge dropped upon us a relentless tonnage of water. Macky, his face ghastly, spun under the pillars of rain. 'My dog! My dog!' he yelled while the heavy squalls slashed at his body.

'What do you mean, your fucking dog?' bellowed Morgan.

'Melly brought him back to me this morning,' shouted Macky. 'He looked fucking great. But I left him outside, tied to his fucking line, Morg.'

'Well, he'll just get wet then, won't he? What 'ou on about?'

'I love that dog, Morg.' Macky was almost in tears.

'Macky, you astound me sometimes,' Morgan said. He pulled his shirt collar tight against the rivulets that streamed through his hair onto his neck. 'Let's get to the Rails before we fucking drown.'

I was absolutely miserable. Already soaked through to the skin. My brace started to creak as the water got into the joints around the heel and ankle. Of course, Morgan couldn't resist that. 'Now Spazzy's old tin leg is squeaking. It'll turn rusty soon and seize up. We'll have to leave him for scrap iron.'

He cackled into the storm.

Macky still shook his head and looked back over his shoulder as if he expected to see something horrible coming out of the shadows. I thought about that gypsy's curse: the one about the dog. I could see Macky eating dog *food*, had seen him crunching up one of them biscuits, but I couldn't see him eating dog *meat*. He had a bizarre way with any animal. But his dog was like some kind of totem to him. Ugly bloody thing too. Like a cross between a wolfhound and a corgi. Big fucking hairy head but its legs seemed too short for the body. To give you an idea about Macky's attitude to animals in general and dogs in particular I can tell you about that time – two summers ago – just before they put Macky inside for stealing the Kawasaki. It was when me and the Mack had spent a long afternoon boozing at his shack. At the end of his garden – not much of a garden, completely fucking barren – there was a ditch. It was full of all kinds of rubbish: bottles, cans, soggy old newspapers, pieces of cardboard. We were sitting on these old crates, see. I had a pile of

68

pebbles and I was trying to toss them inside the rim of an old bike tyre.

'Oh Spaz, wait a minute, mun,' Macky says.

Behind a damp square of cardboard something fluttered. Macky grabbed a stick and poked at whatever was behind it. A big crow hopped out into the open, all shiny black among the rusty tin cans and rotting potato peel. It flapped one wing as it tried to keep its balance, while the other dragged through the slimy effluent in the bottom of the ditch. Right away I was on guard. A fucking crow, like. You can't mess with them. If they weren't fucking spooky they wouldn't put 'em in horror films like, would they?

Macky's dog went nuts, but it was tied to a pulley and cable that hung from a line strung across the backyard which jerked it back before it could snap at the crow. Macky scooped up the bird and pinned the good wing against its body. The other wing hung down. He probed beneath the feathers and ignored the hard beak that jabbed at him.

'Car must have got it, mun. Don't seem to be nothing broken but it's got a nasty gash under here.'

Macky was all tender. I was surprised. He took the bird inside. With water and iodine, I helped him clean the matted wound. The bird shat on the kitchen table.

'Well, there's fucking gratitude for you now, innit?' Macky said.

For days he fed that crow. He gave it syringes full of milk, forcing the beak open with the tips of his tattooed fingers. After a week, it was perky, so Macky dug up some worms from the ditch. Macky strutted around like a proud father when the bird finally tilted its head and lifted a worm, then jerked it down inch by squirming inch.

Macky said, 'I'm gonna teach this thing to fly again, Spaz!'

He set up a tall wooden perch on the waste ground. He tied a cord to the crow's leg. The idea was to pull the bird off the perch and it would have to start flapping.

The dog barked like hell so Macky locked it in the shack. Then he came back and stayed in the garden for hours, determined to make the crow fly. The bird got all ruffled at first. It just dropped like a feathered ball and tried to drag itself away but Macky had it by the cord.

After three days, the crow finally flapped into the air. Six days and it lifted off to glide across to the gatepost. Macky was ecstatic. He took the cord from the crow's leg and let it hop and flutter about in the garden. To my surprise, it didn't want to go anywhere. It was the easy food, I think. But Macky was mightily pissed off when the bird dug into the dog's chow bowl.

'What right does it have, Spaz? That's Bran's grub, innit?'

The crow was in the garden all summer. It pecked around the mongrel and snatched scraps of meat that Macky had flung out there for the dog, after we'd had a Chinese takeaway in the shack. When the dog went berserk, the bird flapped back to the perch.

It was hot that summer. Me and Macky would pass

away the afternoon drinking a few flagons of cider. The crow picked at the dog's bone and hopped out of range when the mongrel snapped at it. Back and fore, back and fore. I never got bored watching them.

'That fucking crow don't belong here, Spaz,' Macky said.

All of a sudden, like. After weeks of training the fucking thing.

'What do you mean, Mack?' I said.

'It's a wild animal, innit? It ought to be wild. Out looking for carcasses and that. All it does is sit around here, torment my dog and eat all his fucking food.'

'Well, it's a crow, Mack. They're scavengers, like. And he's found an easy screw. But it's not a fucking sparrow, you know what I mean.'

'No,' he says.

'Crows are like . . . supernatural, innit? Bring you luck.'

'Bullshit,' he says.

Macky claimed I was off the wall when I said stuff like that. But he believed it himself right enough. He didn't want to believe it, despite the evidence. He hated things he couldn't control. The bird didn't seem to have any inclination to leave.

We heard some kids' voices approaching from down the hill. Three boys, about twelve years old, came by the ditch. They all had bows and arrows.

Macky leaped to his feet, spilling the bottle.

'Hey, son! Gimme that here. Lemme try a few shots.'

I picked up the cider bottle, so's not to waste it. I wiped away the dirt from its mouth and took a warm drink. I had that warm and fuzzy summer buzz on.

A skinny blond kid, frightened, gave up his bow.

Macky notched an arrow.

'Hunting tip. Fucking nice.' He stretched the bow. 'Where's the target, Spaz? Something with a bit of challenge, innit?'

Macky pointed between my feet. I panicked.

'Shoot at the fucking tyre, Mack.'

He looked at me in disgust.

'Throw something in the air,' he says to the kid.

'Can't hit a moving target, mister.' The kid snickered nervously.

'Who can't?' Macky said.

The dog raced at the crow and snapped at it. The bird flapped into the air. Macky spun on instinct. The arrow whacked into the black body. It dropped with a convulsive flutter. A sharp tingling came up from between my shoulder blades and over my scalp.

'Oh fuck,' I said. 'That's bad.'

Macky turned to the kids.

'Who fucking can't?'

If he'd had another arrow, I know they would have been next. So did they. The boys took off down the hill, full tilt.

'Why the fuck did you do that?' I said.

Macky flung the bow into the ditch.

'That bird should have been out of here weeks ago. Nothing and nobody will ever torment my dog and get away with it.'

He went off towards his shack.

Extreme bad vibes had to follow and they did. Two

weeks later, someone left a beautiful Kawasaki 750 outside the Rails. The key was still in it. The owner must have been totally fucked up or brain dead. How could Macky resist a ride on that Kwaka? He couldn't. The trouble was that there was a street full of witnesses, so the next day the coppers came for him, nonchalant like, and arrested him. Macky didn't have a chance in court. He said he couldn't remember where he'd left the bike because he was so drunk. Given his previous, they gave him two years. Karmic retribution for the crow, I thought. But they never found the Kwaka.

Now, back in the present, he had been out of jail for about eleven hours. He was getting drunk. That Kwaka would probably show up again soon.

The rain began to slacken. I wasn't looking forward to sitting around, soaked through – even in the warmest pub – because I knew it was going to take hours to dry out, and it would probably play havoc with my leg. I could already feel the knee get painful as the wind blew against my trousers. My skin turned numb.

Then the rain stopped. The clouds broke up under the spring wind and the moonlight lit up Macky's pale face. I swear it looked like he was tripping. I had a horrible sick feeling in the pit of my stomach. If Morgan felt anything at all he kept it to himself and forged on down the deserted street, eager to reach the pub. It wasn't that far to go. We crossed the bridge by the fire station and went up the hill past the bus terminus. A few skinheads hung around there because they had nowhere else to go.

The alcohol had started to wear off. I thought that

I'd have to have another pint soon just to keep warm. The Rails was just up ahead.

We pushed our way through the etched glass doors into the lounge. The Clash, 'White Riot', blasted from the jukebox, and the patrons yelled at each other over the riffs in order to get themselves heard. It wasn't too full. There was a group of about ten boys in full punk outfit, black boiler suits, hanging straps, black Docs, short hair moussed in spikes. That was about the sum total of punks in Merthyr so far. They sat in a circle around a couple of tables. Melly and four or five of her mates were near the door to the ladies. But no Angela or Maria Grazia. In the far corner a lone figure sat at a small round table. Shadows folded themselves around him. It was my old mate, Harry Williams, Harry Krishna, the Priest. Priest had dressed in black since that fateful day when he had taken some particularly powerful acid that had his number on it. Back then, he had been wearing an outfit of crushed velvet jacket, an embroidered kaftan and multicoloured silk scarves, hence the handle: Harry Krishna. But he told me that he had felt like a walking kaleidoscope on that trip, convinced that the glow of his colours was acting like a beacon to hostile barmen and members of the drug squad. From that day on, Priest had sought invisibility, kept to the shadows and dressed in black. He had largely found it in the obscurest corners of the busiest bars. He looked across the lounge. A spark of recognition lit up above the rim of a full pint.

''Ows it going, Davey?' he said.

I was happy to see him, hoping that things would calm down under his influence. Morgan got a round in. Priest's nickname fitted him perfect. Hardly anyone remembered his former name. With that, and the black jacket, shirt and trousers, people in the town who saw him around assumed that he had once been a real priest, or that he had been thrown out of the seminary for some unspeakable transgression. Priest never did anything to deny the rumours. As others in this town of circus characters had – for their various reasons – cultivated a voluminous knowledge of subjects like gardening, or the American Civil War, or Welsh or British History, Priest had read all he could lay his hands on concerning the history and philosophy of religion. He could reel off the beliefs of the Boro of Brazil, the headhunters of Samoa, the Buddhists of Nalanda and their differences with the Buddhists of Sri Lanka. He knew the intricacies of the Mahabharata, the familiars of the Tungus and Tlingit, the rise and fall of Islam in Spain, its cross-fertilisation with the Cabalists and the Cathars, and its influence on the troubadours and Dante. He knew of the fights of the Jesuits with the papacy, and the ninety-seven points of Luther's proclamation at Wittenberg. I never got tired of listening to him. Well, almost never. He was the only one of us who had been to college, of course. Not that he'd had an easy time of it up in London. In the valleys, he had been in his element. Everybody knew him. Up there, his accent marked him for a foreigner. Everyone he met made some stupid comment about mines or mountains. It turned him bitter. He hated the English. He worked to raise money for the families of the internees in Long Kesh. It might have been money for the IRA for all anybody knows. For a while he got really belligerent and very close to alcoholic. The only worry I had for tonight was whether any of that would come out when Morgan's brother Gerry arrived. Better for Priest if it didn't. He was not a good fighter.

'What are you doing in here then, Priesty?' Macky asked him.

'I thought that maybe I could get laid. The place is usually packed with them schoolgirls on a Friday night, and I wanted to try my luck. But it doesn't look like I'll have much joy tonight. Melly Saunders and her crew are the only ones in here. With those girls' reps I'm a bit wary, Mack, you know what I mean? Never know what you might catch.'

The air seemed to solidify. Macky's shoulder muscles visibly bunched. His eyes narrowed to slits and his lips curled back as he articulated his words, slowly and with difficulty, through gritted teeth: 'Are you calling Melly Saunders a slag?'

Priest looked pained. 'Fuck no, Mack. You know what I mean, mun.'

His voice trailed off, flustered, knowing that if he tried to explain himself it would only make it worse. Macky looked nasty.

'Melly Saunders is an old girlfriend of mine. If I ever hear you call her a slag again, I'll break your fucking back.'

No one doubted Macky's flat statement.

After that little exchange there was more than a moment of silence. Macky and Morgan seemed to take a perverse delight in letting the tension drag on. The record had ended on the jukebox, and the pub hubbub, for some reason, had dropped to a low murmur. Two guys crossed the room and went out through the door, bound for new drinking grounds.

'Hey, Melly,' Macky called.

Oh fuck, I thought, here we go. He was going to tell her what Priest said.

'What 'ou wunt, Mack?'

'Where's that little blonde girl?'

What a fucking relief.

'The barman threw her out. She was arrested in here last week for under-age drinking.'

'For fuck's sake,' Macky said and sat down again.

He gave the barman one of them homicidal looks and I thought that he might at least maim him; but then, just at that moment, a tall, well-built man came into the room. He had the same high cheekbones as Morgan but he had a well-groomed air about him that Morgan would never have cultivated. He was as studiously suave as Morgan was deliberately dissipated. I knew right away who he was, and as he cracked a smile in that hard face, I noticed that he wasn't broken-toothed any more. He must have had his teeth capped.

'Gerry!' Morgan bellowed.

That broke the ice again, and Macky and Morgan were up, all handshakes and back slaps, and doing the old ''Ow's it goin'?' and Gerry was doing it right back. A pint was set in front of the returning soldier which he immediately lifted with a 'Cheers, boys!' and sank a good half of it. Gerry had saved the day for Priest and the fucking barman.

'You all know my brother, boys, don't you?' Morgan said.

Gerry looked blank when he eyed up Priest and puzzled when he looked at me.

'We were in the same class at infants school,' I said.

'Your face seems a bit familiar,' Gerry said, 'but I can't say that I can place it.'

'Davey Daunt,' I said.

He shook his head at first and then it dawned on him. 'Oh, the boy with the bad leg.'

We nodded to each other in recognition and then Gerry turned to Macky.

'What's 'appnin' then, Mack?'

'Not much yet, mun. There haven't been time to find my feet, like. Duw, I haven't seen you this years, Ger.'

'Aye, well, I been busy, like. You have too, so I hear. Sent down for driving a fast motorcycle, wasn't it?' Gerry said.

''Ow come they let you out now then?' Macky asked. 'It's fuckin' Easter. They let the regulars handle it, or what?'

Gerry shrugged. 'Well, they got to give us a day off, now and then, see. My turn this time.'

'You *have* been over in Ireland, haven't you?' Morgan said.

Gerry turned his pint pot around on the McEwan's beer mat.

'Well, we're not supposed to say anything about where we've been and that, you know what I mean, but generally they send us where there's plenty of trouble.'

Macky, to get things cordial, I suppose, said, 'Priest's been over there, too – haven't you, son?'

Priest looked a bit surprised because Macky seemed

so friendly all of sudden. Gerry looked surprised because Priest did not look anything like a soldier. He was short, skinny and dishevelled.

'When was that?' Gerry asked.

Priest picked up at being included in the conversation again but his eyes flicked this way and that. He'd been in Ireland during his political years. I wondered what he'd been up to.

'I was over there when a mate of mine, Jamie Pierce, got married. He was from Armagh.'

The muscles momentarily tightened around Gerry's jaw. Armagh. Bandit country. Everybody knew from the news, innit?

'I was in college with Jamie,' Priest said. 'And he invited me and my girlfriend to the wedding. It was incredible.' I have never seen anything like it over there. You're walking down the street of a housing estate, just like up the Gurnos; suddenly, you see a bunch of soldiers come down the street. They don't just walk down the pavement though. The first one ducks behind a corner and points his rifle down the street. The second one runs ahead and ducks down behind a garden wall. The third one runs on further and hides in a doorway, pointing his rifle. And they go on like that, like a bunch of kids playing commandos. There you are, just walking along normally, and suddenly you've got all these soldiers ducking down in front of you, and around you, and behind you, like a weird play going on in the street.'

'Aye, but if they just strolled down the street normally, they could get shot from anybody's upstairs window,' Gerry said.

'It makes you pretty uncomfortable,' Priest said. 'There's a weird atmosphere, like. You've heard all this stuff on the news about bombings and shootings, and sectarian murders and you don't know what to expect.'

Gerry quaffed some of his beer. It didn't seem like he was anxious to add anything, so Priest continued, as if he felt a need to fill the potential silence.

'We were in this Catholic pub, right, in my friend Jamie's part of town. I'd gone over there with this friend of mine called Monty. We'd brought a bit of dope over for the wedding, like. So, you know how it is. Someone says to his mates, "Those are Jamie's friends from England; knowing Jamie, they've probably got a bit of blow." Next thing you know, Monty comes out of the toilet, white as a sheet. "Gimme the stash!" he says. So I say, "Why? What's the matter?" Monty says, "Just give me the weed. There's a guy in there says he knows we've got some blow. He's in the IRA, and if I don't give it to him right away, he'll have his unit shoot my kneecaps off." Old Monty looked worried, boys, I can tell you.

Priest seemed to lose his train of thought. He glanced across at Melly Saunders and back to the silent soldier.

'Well, what happened?' Macky demanded to know.

Morgan nodded, poker-faced. He gave Gerry the thumbs up as if we didn't exist. Priest came back to himself and carried on the story.

'Jamie was sitting there and he says, "What's the guy look like?" So Monty says, "He's a tall feller with red curly hair and a straggly beard." Jamie just starts laughing.'

Priest was into the story now.

'So Jamie says, "He's a fockin' bullshitter. Just tell the tosser to fock off!" So there's Monty scared shitless that he's going to get kneecapped, and there's Jamie swearing up and down it's a hoax to get the dope, and neither me nor Monty know what's really the truth of it. Anyway, the guy must have got fed up waiting in the toilet, so out he comes. Jamie starts yelling at him, "You leave my fockin' friends alone, Corcoran. There's more than enough of us here to fockin' do you bad." And the guy just shrugs his shoulders, and goes back to drinking with his mates in the next room.'

'That's the trouble, see, boys,' put in Gerry. 'You never know where it's going to come from next, or who's going to do what.'

Gerry didn't look like a man who would be taken by surprise.

'We didn't actually see anything happen, though, you know,' said Priest. 'Not as such. There was no bombs or shootings or anything. Jamie's family was really fantastic to us. They were just over the moon that anyone would voluntarily come over and visit them, with all the trouble that had gone on for so many years. It's just weird, like. There's everything there that you see here: shopping centres, housing estates, the bookies, the pubs; but then you get these checkpoints all over the place, all this barbed wire and that, and these fucking soldiers pointing a gun at your head while they ask you all these questions. But I never seen nothing really. No trouble, like.'

Gerry took a sip of his pint.

'Tell 'em what you told me about that pub, Ger,' Morgan said. 'He's seen some fucking trouble, I can tell 'ou.'

Gerry nodded and put his pint down.

'Well, the first time I was over there, like, they sent all of us new ones on patrol, to get acquainted with what was going on, like. We were driving around Belfast, in this Saracen armoured car. There was about six of us in the back; and it's dark, like. We can hear the radio going, and it comes over that there has been a bombing in a hotel, about a mile away.

'We weren't that bothered, you know. All we planned on doing was turn up and put on a show of looking around, because there's not a lot you can do, is there, after the fact? The Saracen goes through the police cordon. Lights are flashing through the slits in the armour. The driver pulls up and we jump out of the back. We ran straight into the hotel. There's fucking glass everywhere. The place is black from the blast and the smoke, and we got through the lobby and into the bar.

'You wouldn't believe it. All the glass in the place is completely in shards – bottles, glasses, mirrors, everything. There's this horrible moaning of these poor bastards the ambulance men are trying to lift on to stretchers, and these people were lacerated, let me tell you. Some of them have got their skin and flesh hanging off the bone in ribbons. There was blood everywhere. You wouldn't believe the stench. I walked in, just staring, and I put my foot on something that rolled out from under my sole. I nearly fell over. I looked down, and there was this fucking arm lying there, in a torn-up sleeve, and God only knows where the rest of the body was. Then I realised it wasn't the only spare part on the floor.'

'Oh fucking hell,' I said, 'that's fucking awful.'

'They train us pretty well, boys,' Gerry said, 'and they expect us to take anything. I'm not exactly the squeamish type either, but when I saw that floor covered in bits of flesh and bone, and glass and splintered wood, my guts started churning. I just clamped my mouth shut and tried not to spew up in front of the officer. I don't know how many bodies were in there – maybe not many; but the stink of blood and scorched flesh, and burned velvet benches, was unbelievable.

'We poked around a bit, but it was obvious that the only people doing any good in there were the ambulance men. We pulled out and got back in the Saracen, and not one squaddie said a word. "That's what you're up against," said the officer, "so I don't expect any of you to go around pussyfooting when you're dealing with the Micks."'

Gerry quaffed a good third of a pint in one swallow.

'Fucking Prod bombs do the same though,' he said. All nonchalant.

'Another one, boys?' asked Macky, and picked up the empty pint pots to refill them. Morgan and Gerry looked at Priest like two snakes ready to strike.

Back with the pints came Macky, then Gerry had a wicked smile on his face. I know Morgan was eager for another story of carnage and mayhem in Belfast. I'm sure he wanted to freak Priest out. Morgan turned to his brother. 'I heard on the news the other day that they got one of your boys. On an undercover mission, right?'

Gerry nodded. I didn't think he wanted to talk about it.

'Did you hear about that?' Morgan asked me.

I shrugged. 'I never watch the news,' I said. 'It's always the same old bullshit every night.'

''Ow do you expect to know what's happening in the world then, Spaz?' asked Morgan. 'I always know what's going on, I do. Your fucking brain must be about as rusty as your leg.'

I didn't reply. Nothing was going to stop him telling the story anyway.

'It was on the news,' he said. 'There was this soldier doing surveillance work. The army had built a kind of secret compartment in the false ceiling of a laundry van. The IRA got wind of it somehow, and filled the bloody thing with bullets. The bloke above the false ceiling didn't have a chance. He was caught in his own trap, mun. Anyway, the IRA had kidnapped a reporter and they had him there to tell the story, so everybody would know. 'Course, the IRA claimed that the army was using the laundry van for one of their death squads. They said that when the army fingered an IRA suspect, they'd park the van down the street from where he lived and then bump him off as soon as he walked by and there was no witnesses. The Government said it was only a surveillance vehicle. Well, whatever they were doing in the van, who gives a fuck, anyway?'

I could see that Priest was a bit uncomfortable. He sipped at his half. Nobody could normally get a word in edgewise when Morgan was on a storytelling kick, but for a bloke who was supposed to be so secret about his job, I could see Gerry Black was eager to put in his few thoughts on that incident.

Morgan paused for a second to roll a fag and Gerry started right in.

'We tried to pull in the bastards who were responsible for it, I can tell you. We had a sweep of the streets straight away but those boys had disappeared down their rat holes on the estate. We grabbed the reporter and we put the fear of God into him. Then we picked up a few blokes off the street just so they could tell those Taig bastard neighbours of theirs what happens when one of ours goes down on their fucking street.

'We had this bloke, right. I don't think he had anything to do with it, but one of the RUC boys had noticed him gawking at the van, the ambulance men and the coppers, instead of staying off the street like he should have. We grabbed him and gave him a few cracks with the batons when he started to complain. Then we threw him into the back of the Saracen. These kids had turned up now and started throwing stones. Then a few nail bombs. So up come the regular squaddies with the rubber bullets and riot gear to sort 'em out.

'Anyway, we've dragged this bloke off and we got him to the barracks. We took him to the Romper Room. This bloke was scared shitless. We left him with the sergeant, a real nasty piece of work. So the sergeant is acting all nice to him. He gives him a glass of water, and lets him smoke a fag after that. 'Course, he'd spiked the fucking water with acid.'

'What a bastard,' Priest said.

Slip of the tongue, like. Priest hadn't been able to stop himself, had he? Gerry and Morgan both gave him the cold hard stare but nothing more. He was lucky that Gerry, being a loyal member of Her Majesty's Armed Forces, didn't take more extreme exception. But Gerry was well into telling his story: he wasn't going to stop at this point to question Priest's political or moral objections.

'The sergeant starts asking the bloke all these questions about who he is, where he lives, does he have any brothers, does he know anyone in the movement. He keeps repeating the questions over and over. The acid is coming on strong now, and the bloke is getting more and more confused. You could see he didn't know what the hell was going on.

'The idea is you can get them to say anything when they're in a state like that. If they know anyone or anything about the IRA, they'll let you know about it then. Unless they are really hard bastards. It was becoming obvious that this poor bloke didn't know anything at all about anything. He was screaming away and even this sergeant sees that things are getting out of hand; so he says to him, "I'm going to have you do something for me that'll calm you down."

'So the bloke looks a bit relieved. The room is soundproof, right? Apart from the two-way mirror, the walls are all covered in soundboard. You know, the panels with all the holes in them. You can see 'em in record shops. He tells the feller to count every single hole in the room and if he don't come up with the right answer he'll kill him. Then he leaves him on his own. You know the way everything starts to make patterns around you when you're tripping – the poor bastard probably had holes flying round him like a whirlpool because he was trying to grab them to stop them moving. Me and the sergeant was watching him through the two-way mirror. Twenty million fucking holes and he's trying to count them. Then that sergeant sticks his head into the box and says, "Confess, my son, confess."

'The fucking bloke went right off his head. They had to get this doctor in to shoot him up with Valium. We let him go though. Guaranteed, he'll tell everyone on his street what he went through, so they'll all think twice about fucking around with us boys, I can tell you. And they won't be very happy about the IRA using their street for an assassination site.'

Gerry grabbed at his pint. Everything has its place, I suppose, in the universe and that. Good. Evil. Priest looked freaked out and ready to head for the door. Morgan dragged at his fag. Smoke curled out with his words, 'Survival of the fittest, see, boys. That's what it's all about.'

'Listen, Davey,' said Priest, 'I'll see you all later up the Indian restaurant.'

I didn't like to see Priest upset like that. He was my oldest mate.

I said to Priest, 'Hold on a minute now. Let's finish this pint and I'll come with you. They got a nice pint of Brains in the Tankard.'

I didn't want to cut out of the celebration completely so I said, 'Listen, boys, let's meet in the Tankard in an hour or so. Then we can have a nice curry after. There's nothing better for sobering up than a good hot vindaloo.'

'Good idea, Spaz,' said Macky. 'We'll be right behind you. Soon as we finish this pint. Be careful out there. Fucking streets'll be hotting up by now.'

All thought of the gypsies had melted away in the tall tales – but the dread came back in Macky's warning. I felt confused. All those things I wanted to do tonight. Have this celebration. Call up Maria Grazia. I think I was most afraid of doing that. I had the feeling that something was about to go horribly wrong.

Chapter 5

1

Let us turn once more to other players in our drama, players who will act as chorus to the main characters and the armies of mayhem flowing down the valley sides like living rivers heading for their final confluence in the Merthyr High Street, the armies who are, for now, but halfway there and about to come upon a singular Merthyr landmark, the Blaen View.

In the smoke-blown fog and subdued joviality of that Good Friday night, the well-dressed men of the Blaen View sat in clusters in the cramped bar room. Rumbling conversations funnelled and channelled around the room, punctuated by bursts of hilarity that broke staccato through the thickening air. Regulars for close on half a century claimed the various nooks and corners in the closely mapped-out and territorially respected unsaid borders as real as any map in an atlas. The various groups of men made up a continent of tentatively friendly countries forged through the tensions that had originated in the forgotten history of that perpetually darkened room.

From time to time strangers would invade the confines of the pub. They inured themselves to the suffering they caused by the combined powers of wilful ignorance and strong drink. These unwelcome intrusions would usually be fleeting, due to the strangers' lack of loyalty to the pub's numinous ethos or through quiet absorption into the regulars' lives. Those once strangers would find their behaviour inexorably adapting to the unwritten rules of the Blaen View. They themselves would appear as regulars then, and to a man be dressed in well-pressed shirts, ties and suits, or at least a sports jacket and tidy trousers. Roughs were not welcome, especially the stinking and the unwashed. Of course, the occasional well-dressed stranger might be tolerated, if he stood at the bar; even welcomed if he were a regular's guest.

Ben Daunt, my old man, sat in his place on the bench. The same bench he'd sat on every Monday, Wednesday, Friday, Saturday and Sunday night for the past forty-three years barring sickness, accident, or family holiday in parts unknown. The well-polished wood ran into the alcove formed by the front window of the pub with its drawn, tobacco-stained curtains. Ben had stood by his wife over my eviction, but whereas she had sent me to absolute Coventry, he still met me for the odd pint, in here, in this old-time pub, a Welsh longhouse. One of the last. And such is the town, that on that night even Ben and these men were to be caught up in the sweep of violence borne on the winds of riot. As usual, he was accompanied this evening by his stalwart co-religionists, every one with his own undisputed seat. These men's parents and grandparents had left behind famine, strife and poverty in the fields of Ireland and taken the short hop from County Cork to Swansea and thence to the South Wales valleys. The mines and ironworks had claimed these old-time Paddies just as the factories had taken this second generation for its own; but it was the Church that demanded their identity. Across the street from the pub stood that neo-Gothic edifice which had loomed over these men's lives since they first drew breath: the Church of the Holy Martyrs. The very moment of birth had begun the anxious time between their entrance into life and the performance of the rite of baptism. In that interlude, these men had existed as a potential eternal shadow, doomed to the benign part of Hell called Limbo which was reserved for the souls of unbaptised innocents. After the second birth through water, oil and salt, they were co-opted on to the Stairway to Eternal Glory, guaranteed by the stern, and potentially benevolent, authority of the holy Catholic Church; and that set these men subtly apart from their contemporaries in the Welsh valleys. Ben Daunt, Pat McCarthy, Emrys Green and the rest were an integral part of a pyramidal structure that described a process which began with lowly, innocent babes, and proceeded through parish infant school, altar boyship, and successive initiations of the six sacraments of the seven possible that they could choose on their life's path. They were watched over and guided by simple cleric, parish priest, canon, monsignor, bishop, archbishop, cardinal and Holy Father the Pope, and on up to the ethereal realm. There it continued to the angels and the saints, even unto the Most High Authority in Heaven, three aspects in one God, who laid down the certainty of their eternal salvation – if they would but remain within this simple and harmoniously perfect structure. And follow the rules. If not, there gaped the sepulchral entrance to eternal Hell: 'Ashes to ashes, and dust to dust, if God won't have you, the Devil must.' Thus a Redemptorist father to the child Ben. He had never forgotten. For Ben Daunt and his friends, St Patrick's Day had had more importance than St David's Day, at least until the tortured time of adolescence, when they had faced the terrible choice of whom to support on the day that the Welsh International Rugby team had met the Irish at Cardiff Arms Park. The tension of that day summed up the entire conflict of one brought up in the faith of Holy Ireland and Rome, but born on the soil of Wales, in the first generation beyond immigration. The choice Ben had made on that day for the country of his birth had left him haunted and confused, especially as Wales had lost. The pub itself reflected that special consternation. It had two names. The name over the door was 'Blaen View', good and Welsh; but the name by which it was known in the town was the 'Papal Arms'. The design of the flag flying in the garden of the church opposite could have hung on a wooden sign above the pub door, and seemed as normal as any pub sign. The church's banner was halved in yellow and white, with a gold, triple-crowned mitre and crossed keys beneath. Many a town in Wales has pubs called the Crossed Keys, or the King's Arms, or the Triple Crown, and signs to match.

As the church emptied out of a Sunday lunchtime, or from the evening mass of a holy day of obligation, the pub filled up, off-duty barracks and officers' mess of the Church Militant on Earth. They were a power.

A serious political power in the ranks of the Welsh working class.

'And you know what he said to me?' (This was Pat McCarthy's voice.) 'He said, "You're only in it to see what you can get for the bloody priests." I said to him, "Look, I'm doing everything I can to get this school built, because I believe every child should be brought up in their own religion and have the best education. Same as I supported, and fought for, funds for the building of Pen-y-Bont school for non-Catholic children." I told him, "You've nothing to accuse me of. I've never made any bones about it. I've never tried to hide what I believe in. If you ask me if I'm a Labour Catholic Councillor, I'd say, 'No, I'm a Catholic Labour Councillor.' The Catholic has always come first, and the Labour part second; but I'm Catholic to the soul, and Labour to the core, so you can't fault me on any of my record. I'll never have to hide it."'

Pat shifted to the right and left in his chair, visibly agitated, and slightly flushed, as he finished reliving his altercation.

Emrys Green nodded gravely. 'That's right, Pat; always been straight with them, you have.'

'Sorry, boys,' Pat said.

He was obviously embarrassed at his outburst of emotion. That was a sure sign to him of the effect of drink.

The others tacitly ignored Pat's discomfort. One unwritten law of imbibery had been subtly transgressed. These men had trained themselves over the years so that the more alcohol they drank, the straighter they sat up in their chairs, and the clearer they enunciated every syllable as they exchanged their banter. Not a trace of slump or slur or loss of control was allowed to slip into posture or conversation. The men were a picture of perfect physical and mental coordination. If they erred in lack of inhibition, it stayed well on the side of strict decency. Pat had recovered himself, thought about going home, but his tension subsided as he realised he was well on the correct side of control and had stepped but momentarily beyond it.

Johnny Rees, Ben Daunt's oldest friend, didn't ask the other men what they were drinking but lifted the glasses from the bar. The pints were already poured and waited under the eye of the barman who knew these men's habits from long familiarisation. The men raised their tankards as if pulled by the same strings.

'Any word of Davey, Ben?'

'Aye, John, now and then, see. He's well in with those yobs from the Wellington so God knows what he's up to. I dread to think, mun. His big butty just got out of jail. There's a nice sort now. That Macky. He's been in the clink for the last two years. Stole a motorbike or something. And they never bloody found it.'

'Aye, he's a rum bugger that one. Always in and out of Swansea Jail. It's funny how Davey picked up with him, innit?'

'I tell you, John. Davey was never a thief but I'm scared of my life that he'll be with that Macky when the nutter does something he shouldn't, and Davey'll be down with him. By Christ, John, he's gone through his life drifting from job to job and on to the dole. I thought I'd stop worrying, mun, when he grew up. But it's like he never did. I suppose you always worry about your kids. I've had more of my fair share with Davey. And his mother too. She's afraid he'll end up on drugs.'

'Well, if he was going to be a bloody junkie, Ben, he would have done it by now. There's plenty of opportunity round here, innit?'

'Right enough, John, I suppose.'

'I tell you, Ben. Davey's not a bad bloke, you know. But he never liked to fit in anywhere, did he? He probably don't even fit in with Macky and his pals.'

'Aye, but if he's hanging around with them anything can happen, see, John. And they're always in fights. They're famous for it, mun. Macky and that Morgan Black. And you know what it's like down the town these days. It's the bloody Wild West, innit? All them kids out to make a reputation for themselves. It's got worse too. There was always fighters, but nowadays, it's like the whole bloody town has gone stark raving mad.'

There was a sudden bang that rocked the pub. A flash of electric white pierced the cracks in the curtains. The pub lights flickered. In the stunned silence, the crash and rattle of rain shook the glass of the pub's windows. Almost immediately, a wave of laughter rocked through the room.

'I thought the bloody house was coming down,' Johnny said.

'Spring thunder!' declared Pat the Politician.

'That must have been bloody close,' Ben said.

'Aye, the flash and the bang were completely together,' Johnny Rees said.

'Somebody must have been doing something wrong, boys,' Pat said.

The men reached for their pint pots. On the telly, there was a variety show with an orchestra playing a medley of old Beatles tunes. The syrupy strings softly emasculated the rock and roll. Johnny Rees lit a cigarette.

'Another drink, boys?' offered Pat. The other men nodded.

Another crash shattered the quiet of the room. Glass showered from a side window over the men's heads and on to the damp tables. The men ducked away from the flying shards that nicked the skin of the backs of their hands, their only instinctive protection.

'What the bloody hell!' roared Tommy Charles, a red-faced building worker. He'd been on a stool at the bar but now was on his feet, his fists balled as he faced the invisible menace. The wind gusted a squall of rain through the broken window. It billowed the brown-stained curtains. A clean breath of wet night air streamed through the cloying warmth of the smoky bar. Over the steady crash of the relentless rain they could hear the muffled cheers of kids' voices outside in the street.

The builder's eyes bulged.

'They broke the bloody window!' said Dai Ryan the barman.

He grabbed the phone to call the police.

From the dark corner of the bar, two rugged faces emerged into the yellow light. Gary Taft, lorry driver;

the other, Berwyn Evans, now a stacker in the brick factory. They followed the builder to the door.

'Watch out now, boys,' called Johnny Rees, 'there's probably a gang of them. Sodding hooligans!'

The three bruisers went out the door and the regulars followed behind to see vengeance sought and if it would be wrought.

2

Minutes before, the skins had just reached the junction of the Walk with the Brecon Road and they were all over the road between the Blaen View and the grey stone towers and heavy buttresses of the Catholic church. Bugsy and Anto were soaked. Their hands were freezing on the metal handles of a brimming dustbin which they swung between them a–one, a–two, a–three and then sailed it at the window of the Blaen View which shattered upon impact. Kerrraash!!!

That was enough for Bugsy. He was off again at the head of his skinhead army, double-timing it down the Brecon Road towards the high street. But Anto did not move. He stood, wet and bedraggled, with two other stragglers – Shiner and Gobbles – and they waited to see what would happen next.

The bin lay on its side in the broken glass. Its stinking contents had spilled all over the pavement: broken egg shells, dripping cans. The pouring rain flushed sticky sauce into the gutters. Then a crowd of middle-aged drinkers suddenly came spilling out of the pub. At that precise instant, a blinding fork of lightning struck the church spire and the crash of thunder pounded and shook the street. Skinheads and pub patrons ducked as one.

'The cross is toppling off the steeple,' yelled Tommy the builder.

The massive piece of sacred stone split from the tip of the steeple and arced downwards. It smashed through the slates of the rectory.

'You fuckers!' Berwyn yelled.

As if it was Anto's fault. Anto began to back away but before he could turn and run, the burly building worker was upon him. Shiner and Gobbles stood there stunned. Anto twisted free of the brickie's grip but Shiner wasn't so smart. The brickie swung his sledgehammer fist and it slammed into the side of Shiner's head. Shiner's neck snapped back and he hit the wet deck.

Anto called out: 'Get up, Shine!'

But Shiner was down for the count. The other two pub men were slower to reach Anto and he pivoted sharply and exploded into a sprint. Gobbles wasn't as quick off the mark. He was jerked back on his heels as Berwyn Evans, ex-boxer, yanked at the back of the boy's windcheater. Gary Taft slammed into Gobbles with his shoulder and the little skinhead was spun off his feet, suspended by his jacket in Berwyn's tight grip.

'Anto, help me!' Gobbles squeaked.

Anto stopped about twenty yards down the street and saw his friend take a boot in the stomach from the lorry driver.

'Hold on, Gobbles.'

Anto was all instinct. He pulled out a knife that he kept in his jacket. He charged back at the men who flailed and kicked at little Gobbles. Shiner, the first to be decked, was being dragged by the scruff of his neck towards the pub door. Tommy had him in a tight clutch.

'Leave 'em alone, you fuckers!' yelled Anto.

Gary Taft the Lorries turned to face Anto's charge. Anto's hand swung in a wide arc and the thin blade stuck deep into Gary's upper arm.

'Oh fuckin' hell! He stabbed me!' Gary howled.

Gary stared in disbelief at the metal sliver and boyish fist attached to his numb biceps. Anto jerked his knife out of Gary's muscle and staggered back. The ex-boxer methodically continued to punch Gobbles in the face, the body, the face, the body, then relaxed his grip on the kid's jacket and ran forward to help Gary. The lorry driver simply clutched at his gouged biceps and shook his head in disbelief.

'He fucking stabbed me.'

Gobbles struggled to his feet, and hobbled back up the street the way that the skinhead gang had come from. His left eye socket bulged red and purple, and his nose streamed blood over his saturated clothes. He gasped for breath beneath ribs that were bruised and aching. Anto took off at a sprint in the opposite direction. He chased after the Shop Boys who had long since disappeared.

'I'll have you, you little bastard,' called Berwyn.

He turned to help Gary back to the pub. The rain suddenly slackened. Above them, the clouds broke up their inky black bulk to let the moonlight wash across the faces of the Blaen View's incredulous patrons. They did have one prisoner, and they would give him a thorough hiding in the Blaen View before the cops arrived.

3

Linda followed in the wake of the debris: upturned dustbins, broken car aerials, spray-painted swastikas, 'NF', and 'Wogs Out' scrawled on the walls of the terraced houses. On the abandoned dentist's office at the bottom end of the housing estate 'Cardiff City OK' was emblazoned in letters two feet high.

Linda was thinking about the Firm.

Gripper was a skin for the buzz he got scaring straights. Or anyone else for that matter. But Bugsy loved that National Front stuff. He sent away for tacky little pamphlets that claimed the Germans had never killed any Jews. He liked badly printed magazines full of pictures of the Waffen SS and adverts for saw-edged bayonets. Cartoons depicting blacks as gorillas.

'All Pakis are Jews' was sprayed on the side of the next broken bus shelter on the way to town.

Looks like Anto's writing, she thought. About his level of intelligence too.

As she was walking down the Walk towards the Catholic church, a familiar figure hobbled towards her on the pavement. He looked badly hurt. The kid looked pathetic. It was one of the young ones.

'Gobbles. What happened, love?'

'They beat me up. Down there. Those men from the pub.' He sobbed. 'They got Shiner, they did. The cops'll have him now. Anto saved me. He stabbed one

100

of them Catholic bastards. I think he got away. I'm out of it, I am. I'm going home.'

Linda grabbed him by the shoulders. Gobbles kept his head down and wouldn't look at her. The left side of his face was swollen, his eye a slit in blazing red flesh, his cheek mottled black and blue. He started coughing and clutched at his belly and ribs.

'Lemme go, Lind. I got to go home. My old man'll fucking kill me if he finds out about the stabbing.'

Linda dropped her arms from Gobbles' shoulders and he staggered off up the hill, never a glance back. A hundred yards away, Linda saw paunchy men puffing at cigarettes. They paced around the pavement outside the door of the Blaen View.

Hitch a ride in the Black Maria, she thought. Keep Shiner company, innit?

She felt the eyes of the pub men on her. She couldn't see any sign of Shiner. Linda lit another cigarette and ignored the stares. Two skins inside already. She had a moment of dread that made her want to curl up in a ball. God knows what they had already done to Gripper. For the benefit of the straights, she kept her face hard, eyes wide and lips twisted. She had a long night ahead.

A police van screeched around the corner. It lumbered towards her, all braying siren and flashing blue light.

4

My old man had seen enough for the night but he could not go home just yet. Not with the church of his forefathers so obviously ravaged by the falling granite and a mystery as to what damage had been done in the darkened rectory. They were about to find out the damage was not just structural. It ran far deeper than that. And we shall partake of that mystery, a dark mirror within which moved the otherwise unseen forces that were bent on shaping the night.

'The cross off the steeple went right through the rectory roof,' Ben said.

'You can see the hole,' Johnny Rees said.

The clouds had broken up and, through a gap in them, the moon reflected on the wet slates of the gabled house beside the church. A ragged black void seemed to float in the middle of the steep pitch.

'Hey, Johnny,' Ben said. 'Let's go to the rectory and see if they're all right.'

Johnny nodded. 'I'm with you, Ben.'

'Watch out now, boys,' warned Emrys Green, 'those hooligans could be back at any time.'

'We won't be a minute, Em,' Johnny said. 'And we can call a taxi from over there, anyway.'

They crossed the road from the pub and followed the high wall that enclosed the church grounds. They came to a wrought-iron gate in the stone edifice. It creaked open when Ben's hand rested on the hinged latch. They entered a narrow cutting overhung with wisteria and rhododendron bushes, planted by Ben himself, and began to climb the dark steps to the rectory. They could hear the high peals of the housekeeper's voice crying out in panic. There were loud bangs, as if furniture were being overturned. They ran up the last of the steps and Johnny Rees pushed the recessed button that rang the doorbell. Inside the house, there was a sudden dead silence. Then footsteps on the tiles inside. A dead bolt clacked back. The heavy door swung open. The face of Mrs Quinlan, the housekeeper, was all angles — pale and frightened.

'Bless the Saints,' she murmured, barely audible. 'Come in, boys, it's like Hell itself has spilled over in here.'

A voice boomed in the hallway: 'On this night, two thousand years ago, Christ himself descended to Hell and the Earth trembled for his loss at the hands of men. And we're having a repeat performance tonight, boys.'

It was Father Tooley. He stood at the foot of the stairs in a long black cassock. One hand gripped the banister to hold himself steady.

Mrs Quinlan ushered the men in.

'Sure, Father Pine has had a brush with death and is in the kitchen. He's shaken to the marrow, poor soul. Come in and see him, boys.'

'How are you, Father?' Ben asked.

'Ben,' the old man said. His round body wobbled above his tiny feet. 'I'm all right now. I had a little tot of whiskey to help me sleep when that terrible storm blew up. I think the little drink has gone to my head. And poor Father Pine, the lightning nearly killed him.'

'Come on, Father. You can get back to bed, now,' said Mrs Quinlan.

Johnny Rees tried to steer the paralytic priest towards his ground-floor bedroom.

'You'll be fine now, Father, don't you worry.'

The priest straightened himself up and let Johnny

guide him. Ben went with Mrs Quinlan to the kitchen.

At the table, young Father Pine sat in his maroon-and-white-striped pyjamas. Thin blue veins in his face made a tracery under the translucent skin. He held his head in his hands. He mumbled into his teacup as Ben and Mrs Quinlan came in. The wiry hair on each side of the shiny bald dome was twisted into little peaks that pointed in every direction. He looked up at Ben through the thick lenses of his spectacles.

'It missed me by inches, Ben,' whispered the young man. 'Mrs Quinlan, would you mind leaving us alone for a few minutes?'

The obedient housekeeper shuffled out of the room. Ben sat down, lips tight and blanched.

'Ben, I can talk to you man to man, now, can't I?' asked the priest.

Ben nodded his head gravely. He had a deep sense of dread. The truth was that he would have preferred not to be talking man to man with Father Pine. He found people revealing their intimate secrets extremely uncomfortable, especially if they were priests.

'Ben, I know your faith is strong, so what I'm going to tell you shouldn't do any harm.'

Dear God, make it quick and simple, Ben thought.

Father Pine stopped suddenly and looked around the room. 'Forgive me, Ben,' he said. 'I should have had Mrs Quinlan make you a cup of tea.'

Ben shook his head. He wished the priest would stop dragging out the agony. 'Don't worry about that, Father, a cup when I get home will be more than enough for me.'

'Well, let me tell you what happened then. You see, Father Tooley was in the study reading his breviary. He'd had a drop of whiskey, and sometimes you know, he forgets himself and pours a little too much. Mrs Quinlan noticed that he was starting to nod off in the armchair and she asked Father Doran and myself to get him to bed.

'These are not happy days for us in the rectory, Ben, as I'm sure you've seen when you've been here doing a bit of work for us and all. I don't know what it is with him, but Father Doran refused to come and help. Well, Mrs Quinlan and I got Father Tooley to bed. I could hear Father Doran stomping around in his room. I told Mrs Quinlan to be off to bed herself but, bless her heart, she said she'd go when she had straightened up the kitchen. So anyway, Ben, I retired upstairs to my room.

'It has been a hell of a strange night. When I got into bed, I tried to compose myself with prayer, but I had such strong carnal desires that it was if the Devil himself was overseeing my torment. And all that despite the austerities of the stripped church and the Good Friday rite. You understand now, don't you, Ben? You won't be too shocked. Sure, we're all men and human at that.'

Ben didn't know if he should shake his head or nod it. My old man hated to talk about anything to do with sex at the best of times. A priest talking like that really upset him. They were supposed to be above it.

'I could hear the snores of Father Tooley below me,' Father Pine said. 'The clatter of plates in the kitchen as Mrs Quinlan tidied up; and I could hear Father Doran talking to himself. I was worried about the man, Ben, but it was as if I was paralysed, caught as I was in the struggle between prayer and sinful thought. Then the first clap of thunder hit us. It was a shock, surely. The whole house rattled. But then a silence descended inside and it seemed like a blessed calm was now restored by the cleansing rain. I lay there peacefully in my bed.

'I was just settling down to sleep when I heard a terrible moan from Father Doran's bedroom. Then there was another clap of thunder and the next thing I knew, Ben, was that something came crashing through the ceiling and landed not a foot from where I lay. It was a great hunk of stone in the shape of the Holy Cross that was lying on the floor like a granite accusation.

'Mrs Quinlan came running up the stairs and without a thought burst through the door. She was very sweet, the dear woman. I staggered out of bed. She looked at the mess, and at me, and said, "Praise the Saints, Father. Will you look at that?"

'I said, "I'm safe, Mrs Quinlan. But I'm afraid for Father Doran." Why I should have been afraid for Father Doran, I have no idea, I'm sure. Perhaps I just didn't want even to consider the brush I'd just had with death. Mrs Quinlan followed me down the corridor. There was no sound from Father Doran's room, so we knocked on his door. Down below, Father Tooley could be heard as he blustered about in his room and knocked over the furniture.

'There was no answer from Father Doran, so I reached down for the doorknob and turned it quietly. I swung open the door and there he sat at his desk, making a noose — from the rope that he used to tie around the waist of his cassock in the fashion of the Benedictines.

'"Father Doran," says I, "what is it that you are doing?" He looked at me with a stare that seemed fuelled by all the fires of Gehenna. And he says, "Judas Iscariot has been discovered. With no millstone tied around the neck at birth and merciful death by water, then all that's left is the noose, Father Pine."

'I don't know to whom he was referring: if this Judas was supposed to be me, or Father Tooley, or Father Doran himself, or even if he had anyone in mind at all. You know, Ben, that he was taking tablets for his nerves. Sure, it had happened to him once before, when he taught at the boys' boarding school. It was a terrible strain on him. All those young boys. He suffered from delusions and was apt to lose his grip. They thought that he had recovered but now Mrs Quinlan and I could see that he'd had a relapse. It shook me every bit as badly as the granite cross on the carpet.

'Mrs Quinlan was immediately quick with a cup of tea. She had found the sedatives which, thanks be to God, quietened him down no end. She's called Dr Donleavy.'

Ben shifted in his seat. They were human, these men, all too human. But that rarely interfered with the course of their duty. And they were assailed upon all sides by Satan. And especially so on this night.

'Well, everything seems to be under control now then, Father,' Ben said.

Father Pine looked at him in surprise. 'I'd like you to come and see if he's all right, Ben.'

Ben went as pale as the priest.

(My old man told me that he felt as if he were somehow being tested. He told me that later, about six months later, when we had both drunk about eight pints each in the Papal Arms.)

Ben nodded. 'All right, Father.'

Father Pine got up from the kitchen table and the two men shuffled into the hall. They began to ascend the wide wooden staircase. There was a smell of varnish and Ben saw his own reflection in the dark of the door panels. Father Pine knocked on the door and turned the knob to enter.

Father Doran had his back to them. He was slumped forward on a straight-backed chair and was staring at his empty palms.

'Are you all right, Father?' Ben asked.

The seated priest stiffened. His fingers curled. His voice came slow and deliberate but it was not Ben to whom he addressed himself.

'We have found our Judas all right; but who, Ben Daunt, will be the Christ tonight?'

(I'm glad that I hadn't heard this conversation at the time. It put the willies up me enough when I heard it after the fact.)

'Father Doran, is there anything we can do for you?' Ben said.

'I'm beyond help, Ben,' came the reply.

He turned to face my old man. There was a cold blaze in the priest's eyes. It was alive behind the glazed cast caused by the mild tranquilliser. Ben Daunt felt his own head spin. He could hear Johnny Rees calling to him from downstairs. The doorbell rang. The faint voice of Mrs Quinlan called out that she would answer it. There with the lunatic priest, both Ben and Father Pine stood aghast, powerless before the absence of reason.

The front door opened and they heard the bluff voice of Dr Donleavy. Then Johnny Rees and the doctor were on the stairs. Ben and Father Pine hung suspended in the mad gaze of the stricken priest who seemed to regard them from the bottom of a pit. Johnny and the doctor came into the room.

'Dr Donleavy's here,' Johnny said. 'I got Father Tooley off to bed. Are you all right, Father Pine?'

'Sure, I'm fine, Johnny,' whispered the priest.

Johnny sank into silence. There was the creak of the doctor's footsteps on the boards.

'I'll take care of him now, boys.'

Dr Donleavy placed his black bag on the dishevelled bed. He took out a hypodermic, all steel needle and shiny glass. He slid the business end into a small bottle and sucked the liquid into the brittle chamber.

'You'll be fine now, Father Doran,' he said.

5

And before we return to the doings of yours truly, one part of our story has to be put to bed even at this early juncture, coinciding as it does with the summoning of the last players to our drama's stage. Let us return to the great concrete-and-glass redoubt of Merthyr police station where one Sergeant Forbes has knocked on Superintendent Sykes's door and entered. Forbes was a quiet man, an old-time copper on the verge of retirement. He looked like a skinny Dixon of Dock Green, balding, grey hair, shadows in the folds of his drooping jowls.

'What is it, Forbes?'

'We've got a spot of trouble, Super. A gang of skinheads. There's been a stabbing outside the Blaen View.'

The super was in his late forties. Pursuing a rapid career through the ranks which did nothing to alleviate his blood-pressure problems that even now caused his face to darken to a deep shade of reddish purple. He had a full head of hair though, the grey at the temples darkened and kept in place by a liberal dose of Vitalis.

'Blaen View!' the super said. 'There's respectable people in there. How many men have we got available?'

'No more than ten or fifteen, Chief, even if we bring in all the patrols off the estates. There's about fifty or sixty in the skinhead gang and they're all pumped up like a soccer crowd. If they get to the bus station, they might get the Bus Boys joining them. That could put it up to eighty or ninety of them.'

'Any of our boys tied up?'

'PC James and PC Williams have got a perp for breaking the pub window, but it's not the one who did the stabbing.'

'Breaking the window but not the stabbing. Bravo, boys. Who else we got around?'

'Sergeant Thomas and that new boy, Phillips. They're doing an interrogation on some skinhead down the hall, but he wasn't with the gang in town.'

'What they got him for?'

'Thomas is trying to get a confession out him for throwing a stone at Phillips' car.'

'Any witnesses?'

'No, sir. Even Phillips doesn't know if the boy did it. It happened when he was passing the Gurnos shops.'

'That Thomas can be a prat sometimes, Forbes. Trying to impress the new kid, I expect. Tell them to get rid of the little fucker. Call everyone in. We'd better break this gang up before anyone else gets hurt. I'll put in a call to the SPG in Ponty. We'll have a vanload of those boys up here, just in case. We'll see if they can earn their bloody keep.'

'I'll get right on it, Chief.'

Forbes moved quickly down the corridor to get a message to the dispatcher. He'd deal with that first and then round up the men in the station. There now, the last brigade was about to be summoned. All was in place for the final Armageddon. Forbes passed the door to the interrogation room.

6

In that interrogation room, Gripper was saying nothing. It was not that he had much idea about his right to stay silent but he had just decided to grind it out and wait till they officially arrested him and then he could get bailed out. Or until they let him go. That had happened often enough in the past.

Sergeant Thomas's ugly red face was about two inches from Gripper's own, and as the copper screamed his demands, Gripper was disgusted by the little flecks of spittle that flew from the policeman's mouth and spotted Gripper's cheek and nose. He had long stopped hearing what the sergeant was yelling. Gripper was just watching out, ready to brace himself for when the maniac punched him in the kidneys or smacked him across the head with his forearm.

PC Phillips was squirming. He was trying to play the good cop, as he had been taught in training, but his heart wasn't into forcing a confession out of Gripper. He didn't really care any more whether Gripper had thrown a stone at the car or not. All it had caused Phillips was a little fluster and embarrassment. This third-degree treatment seemed a bit ridiculous.

Gripper heard another voice in the echoing room.

'Sergeant Thomas, PC Phillips, the super wants to see us all in the ops room.'

Sergeant Thomas spun round. 'What about *him*?' he demanded. He jerked his thumb in Gripper's direction. Forbes motioned Thomas over and they began whispering together. Gripper kept his head down and an eye on Phillips who stood in front of him in obvious discomfort. Gripper wondered if the young cop wanted to take a piss, shifting as he was from one foot to the other. Gripper tried to make out the mumbling that was going on by the door, but caught only 'super', 'skinheads', and 'SPG'. The last letters made Gripper perk up.

When the desk sergeant went out, Thomas came back. He leaned over the table, and with a voice full of venom that Gripper had no reason to believe was false, the police sergeant said levelly, 'I'm going to get you, Gripper. I am going to cause a lot of suffering in your life; and I am capable of doing it. Do you understand?'

Something churned in Gripper's stomach. With those few flat words, Thomas had scared him worse than all the screams, punches and spittle sprays of the attempted intimidation of the last two hours. Despite himself, Gripper nodded his head once, and he knew that Thomas could smell the bowel-loosening fear that Gripper was so desperately trying to hide. Small town, nowhere to go, and a vindictive bastard copper who would give him no peace.

'Now get the fuck out of here,' said Thomas. 'You've been saved by some bloody nonsense on the High Street that we have to take care of.'

Gripper looked around, bewildered. Phillips looked relieved.

'I'll take him out, Sarge,' offered Phillips.

Gripper stood up and Phillips guided him out of the room. They walked down the corridor to the front door, a tense silence between them. Gripper could feel that Phillips was keeping his distance but he recognised that the young copper wanted to say something to him. They reached the door.

'Watch yourself, Grip,' Phillips said.

Gripper didn't turn around to acknowledge him but walked straight down the steps. Phillips disappeared back into the police station. Gripper looked up and down the street, dark and empty, street lights yellow, and glistening the wet tarmac. A girl called his name. Gripper spun around. Linda stepped out of a doorway, twenty yards down the street.

'Fuckin' hell,' whispered Gripper. 'What a fucking night!' Then he shouted: 'Hey, Linda! What's going on?'

Linda came up to meet him. Gripper felt awkward. He didn't know if he should hug her, like he felt like doing, or keep a distance which, he thought, most of his mates would expect him to do. Linda made it easy. She grabbed his forearms, and then punched him lightly in the chest.

'They just let you out, Grip?' she laughed.

'What a pair of prats those two were,' said Gripper shaking his head. 'I don't know why they let me go. I thought I was in there for the night.'

Linda held on to his arm as they went towards the shopping centre. Gripper liked that.

'Where's the rest of them?' he asked.

'Bugsy got them to stir up a bit of aggro, up on the estate. They were coming down town but I don't know where they are now. I came down here the back way, through Georgetown.'

'So you're the only one who come to help me out, is it, Lind?'

'I just waited, Grip. I didn't know what to do really. I just stood in the doorway. I thought about asking at the desk for you, or trying to get a solicitor or something, but I didn't know what to do. I didn't want to make more trouble for you so I waited to see if they'd let you go first, before doing anything.'

'Well, at least you hung around here, Lind, looking out for me. More than those other bastards done.'

'Why don't we go into town, and see what's happening, Grip?'

Gripper shrugged. 'I've had enough for tonight, Lind. I been punched, spat on, and screamed at all fucking night. I jest want to have a rest, mun.'

Linda squeezed his arm. 'Let's go up my house. My mam and dad are probably in bed by now.'

'All right, sounds great,' said Gripper, wondering at his chances for more sex. 'I just want some peace and quiet for five minutes.'

They climbed the concrete steps that led up to the flats above the shopping precinct and the bridge across the river.

'Listen,' said Gripper.

Above the noise of the swollen brown river pouring over the concrete weir, they could hear a distant chant coming from the bus station.

'It must be Bugsy and the Shoppers hooked up with the Bus Boys.'

Gripper felt an urge to be with them again, bouncing in a crowd down the street. If Thomas was going to be there though, and the SPG, Gripper knew he would be a marked man. He also had Linda on his arm and he liked that. He really did. They hadn't broken their stride, heading across the bridge towards Georgetown.

'I like you, Lind,' Gripper said.

As they reached the other side of the river, unbeknown to them, one of the millions of Gripper's sperms – which had been struggling for hours against the force of gravity, or dying as they swam in confused spirals, or leaking out into Linda's panties, or racing against a myriad rivals – successfully connected with the perfect egg that awaited it and began the process that was to result, nine months later, in the birth of a baby girl endowed with Gripper's incomparably robust health and Linda's inquisitive and incisive brain. All this was a lifetime away from where they were now.

They heard a crashing of glass in the distance. The distant sound of those skinhead bastards who were soon to meet up with me and Priest.

Chapter 6

1

Merthyr High Street was busy with Friday-night pedestrian traffic, pub migrations in full force. I think that me and Priest were both glad to be gone from the miasma of violence that clung around Macky and the Black brothers.

''Ow's it going, Priest?' I asked, trying to be sympathetic.

'A'right, son. Can't complain, see.' He sighed. 'Macky, mun, he just don't get it.'

'You know how he is. He's a bit on edge. Just outta jail, innit?' I said.

'Well, listen, Dave, he should take it out on someone who don't like him. Not his fucking mates, like.'

I nodded. Right enough, but hey, it's Macky, innit? What can you do?

Sparse drops spattered on the pavement. Rain glistened on the road ahead and reflected the amber of the street lights. We turned the curve in the road just after the Con Club and the Tankard was a few doors up on the left. We pushed our way into the pub. A number of flushed faces smoothed by the razor's edge crooked back over jammed shoulders to see who had entered. The heads seemed to float above the thick crowd of backs that formed a wall of jackets and pullovers beneath the smoke-filled air. The light was muffled under the red paisley lampshades. Well-dressed young women held on to half-pint glasses of lager, talking among themselves while their spouses exchanged banter about football, rugby and jobs. I felt awkward, out of place. A number of old acquaintances nodded to us and went back to their conversations.

Jeff Dodge, a balding, corpulent ex-rugby player, noticed me.

'Davey, mun. Your brother was just in here,' he said.

My brother. Fuck, I hadn't seen him in weeks. I got on all right with my brother. He was sensible. Married. No kids yet but he had a good job. We'd have a pint together now and then, and he would fill me in on what was going on with the old man and the old lady.

'He say where he's going?' I asked.

'If I know him he'll be up the Gynlais Arms till later. They never fucking close up there, so you got plenty of time, son.'

'Thanks, Jeff,' I said.

My brother. I wouldn't have minded seeing him. I could use him as an excuse to get free of Macky and Morgan. Even of Priest. Then I could telephone Maria Grazia.

The Gynlais, I thought. Maybe later.

Priest was already pushing his way into the fray but Jeff wanted to talk a bit.

''Ow's it going then, Dave? I haven't seen you this ages.'

'Oh, not so bad, mun,' I said.

'In the Welly now, innit?'

'Anywhere, mun.'

'Duw, never in here though, is it?'

'Well, I'm here now, in' I?'

'Fair enough, son.'

'Look after yourself, Jeff,' I said.

I pointed at my drinking butty. 'Priest's on a mission,' I said.

'All right, see you later, Dave.'

I slid after Priest between the backs of two groups of blazered rugby boys. He was negotiating for a possible spot to sit down in the far corner. There was a small gap on a bench by the public telephone next to a group of well-washed apprentice drinkers, just out of school. I got through the crowd to join him.

'Shift up for my mate here, boys,' said Priest.

He knew a few of them, it seemed. The boys looked disgruntled but moved along the bench far enough to give me and Priest room to sit down – a rare opportunity at this time of the evening.

'You have to hear his confession, do you, Priest?' joked one of the boys.

'Watch it now, Dilwyn, or next time you go to confession you'll have no absolution. "Whose sins you shall forgive, they are forgiven. Whose sins you shall retain, they are retained." Move up, now.'

I sat down next to Priest. 'Where are the boys who used to drink in here then?' I asked him.

'They don't come out much now, son. All married off, most of them. Or they go up the Gynlais, where it's quiet.'

'Can't say I blame them,' I said. 'Full of little kids in here now, innit?'

'We're all getting on, see, Dave. New batch every year, innit? The ones old enough probably even vote Conservative by now.'

'Things change, Priest, right enough.'

'Do want a pint?'

'Aye, Brains'll do.'

Priest stood up from the table and threaded his way through the bodies to the bar. He pulled out a damp five-pound note and waved it at the barman. As Priest set down our pints, the boy called Dilwyn decided that he would try to bait him.

'Are you coming to the match on Monday, Priesty?'

'What match is that, son?'

'Catholics versus Protestants, up on Ridley's field. Daunt's brother is captain of the Catholics.'

Priest raised an eyebrow to me. I shrugged.

'What's there to interest me in that?' asked Priest.

'Oh, I thought you were the big religious buff,' the kid said.

'Whose side are you on, boy?' Priest asked.

'I'm a Catholic, in' I?' he said. 'You should come and support your team, mun. You can give us all a blessing.'

Priest laughed. 'You want more than my blessing, son, to win that game. You want some decent foot-ballers like those Protestant boys.'

'I don't expect your blessing's got any power in it now, Priest, eh? I heard you was defrocked. Having the altar boys behind the sacristy, wasn't it?'

Priest raised an eyebrow. 'My differences with the

Church are purely philosophical, my boy. No Papal Bull for me. I know a bit too much about God's instrument on Earth. I could make a parish priest doubt his faith. So don't be talking to me now, if you want to have your eternal salvation.'

'I go to church every Sunday, Priest. Old St Peter will have to let me in,' he replied.

'If you're as good at prayer as you are at football, it'll be Old Nick, not St Peter, who'll be letting you boys in,' Priest said.

'Where's your loyalty, Priest, saying things like that? No wonder you was thrown out. I see you still have to wear the old black robes though, son.'

The boy was struggling.

'You can take a man out of the priesthood but you can't take the priesthood out of the man.'

One of the schoolkids stirred from behind the others. Neither me nor Priest had noticed him before. He looked bleary-eyed as if he had just woken up from being passed out.

'I don't like you, Priest.'

He slurred his words slowly, so that everyone could understand.

'Come on now, Kieran, we're only having a laugh, mun,' said Dilwyn.

'I don't like him, and I don't have to, like.'

The boy was drunker than his mates. He leaned forward.

'I'm a Catholic, I am; and I don't want you running down my Church.'

Priest took a sip of his pint and looked at me.

'I've heard stories about you, Priest,' the boy said.

121

'You're not fit to be in here. Look at you – drinking and carrying on like you do. You're a disgrace to the priesthood. No wonder they threw you out. The bloody least you could do is stay at home and out of the pub so that people don't give the religion a bad name.'

The boy gripped the edge of the table and it rocked as he shifted his unsteady weight. Beer slopped out of the glasses. His friends grabbed the table top to hold it steady and stop any major spillage.

'You're a fucking disgrace!' spat the drunken boy.

'Less a' that now, Kieran!' Dilwyn said. 'We're only fooling around; so fucking leave it out!'

'I think he's had enough, boys,' said the barman, strolling over casually.

Kieran reeled in his seat. I saw the realisation come into his face that his time was up in this pub; and if he wanted to enter it again it was better for him to leave.

'I'll take care of him, Jack,' Dilwyn said. 'Hey, sorry, Priest. We didn't want to cause any bother, mun.'

Young Kieran scowled as his friends dragged him to his feet. He shook them off and made for the door. The others followed him out, making their embarrassed way through the crowd.

'Fucking crazy, innit? I've never been a real priest and some drunken little yob wants to call me a disgrace.' Priest shook his head.

'Well, why didn't you tell him that instead of letting him carry on?' I said.

'Well, it's none of his fucking business what I am,

is it?' Priest said. 'Anyway, you have to keep a sense of mystery about you, see, son.'

I downed my pint and Priest did likewise.

'Fancy a pint up the Gynlais?' I asked him. 'Jeff Dodge said my brother went up there.'

The Tankard, it wasn't my favourite pub anyway, but it felt a bit sour in there now.

'What about Macky and Morgan?' asked Priest.

'Fuck it, mun. They'll find us soon enough.'

2

On the street, four schoolkids reeled over the pavement. Three of them struggled with the other.

'Come on now, Kieran, let's get you home, son,' Dilwyn said.

Kieran shook off the hands that gripped him under his arms. He staggered forward.

'Don't fucking touch me!' he yelled, spluttered. He wrenched himself free. 'Leave me alone, I don't need you fuckers!'

Dilwyn pursed his lips, shook his head. He watched Kieran lurch off at an unbalanced run up the glistening high street.

'There's no stopping him, boys,' Dilwyn said. 'There's no sense in him at all.'

His mates slouched together, not knowing what to do.

'Sod this!'

Dilwyn took the lead again. 'Let's go get the bus home, boys.'

They turned instinctively towards the bus station, dejected by their poor showing in the critical social proving ground of the pub. Kieran was lost to them. They didn't watch him any more as he careened up the high street.

To Kieran, sounds echoed. Cars ran by. Lights burst from shopfronts. His vision swam. Jostling bodies filled the whole street with noise and movement. Chants that he couldn't make out the words of. He sensed the hostility in the unknown faces on the shaven heads that swarmed towards him. Two, three, four skinheads registered sudden recognition of him. A phlegmy voice burst across the rising chant: 'It's Kieran!'

He had suddenly ceased to be prey for the violent wave that surged around him, lifted him up and back. He momentarily sobered as he realised how narrowly he had escaped being pounded to a bloody jelly. He couldn't utter a sound as he found himself spinning around and propelled back in the direction he had come from. His legs churned as his body was carried along in the crush of the crowd. He recognised some of the Shop Boys. But there were others too: the Pentrebach Boys, the Swansea Road Boys, the Bus Boys. It was an army of skins.

He saw Bugsy bump through the bodies towards him. A manic lucidity cut through Kieran's alcoholic confusion. If Bugsy hadn't recognised him, Kieran would have been hospital meat by now. He looked down the street. About thirty yards away he saw a man in black and another with a limp. Guess who? We were far from the safety of the Tankard. We faltered. We searched hastily for a place of escape.

124

Kieran was drunkenly attuned to the fact that the mob of skinheads was eager to go off: to destroy in violent ecstasy any living thing in their path. There was an uncanny, split-second lull in the raging chants and Kieran screamed: 'Those are the bastards who had me thrown out of the Tankard!'

3

Up ahead of us, a rhythmic chorus of voices, steady as an express train, suddenly roared in the narrow tunnel of the high street.

'Oh fuck,' I said. 'Look at that.'

About fifty yards away, a crowd of gangling bodies spun and wavered, filled the whole street with noise and movement, a swarm like a football crowd.

I heard: 'Fucking Greebos!'

And the front rank of skinheads stampeded towards us.

We were slow to react but I grabbed Priest by the arm and pulled him back into a narrow shop entrance, our only immediate hope of survival. And then they were on us. Arms and one foot up, both of us desperately defended our heads and bodies from a rain of flailing fists. Boots swung at us in the confines of the doorway. I stamped down to block them with my good foot and balanced on the braced one. Hands grabbed at us trying to pull us into the open. Before us bobbed these heads all shaved and grey, lips twisted and eyes agoggle, voices screaming, 'Bastards, bastards, kill the bastards!'

Me and Priest lashed out at anything and everything in front of us. It was total panic. We didn't stand a fucking chance. Blows and kicks came into the narrow space and we blocked them with our arms and legs or they thumped into our exposed ribs. I couldn't even feel the pain, I was so pumped up. A fist smacked against the side of my head and knocked all the alcohol out of me. It all seemed so fucking absurd at that point I almost gave up. Then luckily one of the skins spun around in front of the crowd and fell, his arms and legs flapping beneath the feet of the mob. A group of charging skins trampled over his squirming body and lost balance. They tumbled into the jostling front line and fell over each other in a mass of tangled limbs. It let me catch my breath.

In the doorway, me and Priest stood poised to defend ourselves against a renewed attack. I gasped lungfuls of air. My bruises throbbed, the pain still dulled by the adrenalin that surged through my body. I glanced at Priest. He had this stupid grin on his face and he shook his head at me. Then the whirlwind of faces, fists and feet reappeared in front of us. Here we fucking go. At that moment the whole crowd lurched violently sideways as if hit by some phenomenal impact. I heard the crack of bone. The skinhead onslaught stopped as suddenly as it had started. Now, a score of skinheads stumbled over each other. Others tried to regain their feet. It was Macky, Morgan and Gerry who spun among the skins and punched out at anyone who came within reach. Macky was in a hot and murderous frenzy. His face was so distorted that I could only see his left eye glaring like a black lamp and his right eye not at all.

The flesh of his face had twisted upwards. The jagged teeth gaped in the red hole formed by his drawn-back lips. His fists pumped like pistons. He hammered against the pimply faces that appeared before him, dazed and mesmerised. It seemed almost comical, to tell the truth – despite the screams, the smack of impact, the long strings of blood, the flying snot and saliva.

Macky roared from his guts. He grabbed bodies and flung them around like dolls. He was laughing. A horrible bestial laugh. Gerry was a simple efficient fighting machine. Each thrust-kick lifted a boy from his feet and dropped him breathless on the street. For six feet around where he stood, the ground was empty. Each punch left another boy motionless. The skinheads were too recently out of childhood, just too far short of their prime, to stand before these three hard cases. Macky, Morgan and Gerry had a power that came from years of hard street fighting, the prison yard, or the best training in the arts of violence that Her Majesty could offer her military elite. One day, one or two of the mob all around them might reach that dubious peak, but they weren't there yet.

Bugsy's voice yelled out: 'Stop, boys! Stop!'

The skinhead fever suddenly drained away.

Bugsy knew who the horde faced. Morgan lived in the street next to his own. Everyone was aware of Macky's reputation. Gerry he only knew by sight, but his cool and chilling presence and relaxed stance among the bodies that crawled away scared Bugsy as much as the two he knew. There were probably enough skinheads to take the three men if they joined together again and rushed them, but the buzz had gone. Even the youngest and the craziest of the skins knew that they would be hunted down individually and suffer a pitiless revenge if they dared to lift a finger to the men in front of them.

'Come on, boys,' said Bugsy. 'Those fellers must have been friends of Morgan's.' Bugsy tried to save face, to crack a joke. 'Any friend of yours is a friend of ours, innit, Morg?'

'Get the fuck out of it,' Morgan snapped, 'or I'll break your fucking neck.'

Bugsy began to walk in the direction that the men had come from. A few skinheads followed him. Others still milled around confused. The wounded limped or crawled towards the opposite side of the street. The girls and some of the younger boys helped the injured skins to get up. Some of the bleeding were little more than children.

'Come on, boys,' called Bugsy. 'Let's go down the bus station.'

The majority of the skinheads began to move off after him. They gave the men near the doorway a wide berth.

Me and Priest came out of the narrow doorway. Up in the distance, a blue light was flashing on top of a parked panda car.

'Thanks, boys,' said Priest. 'I thought we were goners then.'

'You're always getting into trouble, Priest,' Macky said, 'and you can't fight even to save your fucking life.'

Priest was pale and silent. I didn't have a mirror to see my own face.

'You OK, Spaz?' asked Macky.

I nodded. Nobody even expected me to be a good fighter. That's the crack with the brace, innit?

'Come on, boys. You probably need a brandy after that,' Gerry said.

I felt my lips curl into something like a smile. I could feel my nerves start to vibrate. 'Thanks, Gerry. I reckon I probably could.'

Down the street, we could hear a chant starting up again. The panda came towards us. Macky ignored it and walked in the direction of the Gynlais. The police car stopped again and the officer got out. He was young, about twenty-two. He came around the back of the car towards Macky, and Macky stopped to look at him.

'I could bring you all in for causing a disturbance, you know that, don't you?'

Macky looked at the policeman.

'We stopped a fucking disturbance, didn't we, while you were sitting in the fucking car.'

'You're a pretty tall bloke,' said the policeman, trying to change the subject.

Macky looked down at him.

'No,' he said flatly, 'it's just that I'm standing up here on the kerb and you're in the fucking gutter.'

With that, he walked off towards the Gynlais, and the rest of us followed him towards another round of drinks.

4

My brother wasn't in the Gynlais. The barman said he had left with his wife and another couple. Gone to the Taj Mahal restaurant. It was too early to eat and it would fuck up my timing for Maria Grazia if I went and searched him out. The truth was, I wanted to be on my own for a minute anyway. Be free of Priest and Macky and Morgan and Gerry and the fucking skins and everybody else except maybe Maria Grazia.

I gulped at the brandy. It was like nectar that coated my throat. For a second it took my attention away from the throbbing above my ear. Then I put my fingers there to trace the shape of the swollen egg on my skull. It was a beauty. My shins burned where the skin had been scraped off. I laughed at the way my ribs ached. Perhaps I was in shock.

I pointed at the balloon glass and nodded towards the others. The barman had poured five more brandies for us before I reached the bar. That was the beauty of the Gynlais.

'Did you see the way those fuckers went down?' Morgan laughed.

'Aye, they never knew what hit 'em,' Macky said. 'Just fucking amateurs, innit? That Bugsy's a boy though. He'll be something to reckon with in a few years.'

It hurt to laugh but I couldn't help it. Priest looked awful.

'It's too fucking quiet here, boys,' said Macky. 'Let's go up the Pentwyn End. Tom should be warming up on the piano by now.'

'Naw, he's into the old cajun accordion now, son,' drawled Morgan.

'I never liked it in here, boys,' Gerry shrugged. 'Full of bloody grandads, mun.'

'Fuck, I wouldn't mind a bit of music,' Priest said.

'Boys, I'm not moving from this seat until I can't feel any more pain,' I said. 'You all go on up. The curry house is next door. I'll see you in there at closing time. You can bring Tom and his accordion with you.'

Priest looked disappointed.

'You'll only go get yourself in trouble, Spaz. Stay with us, mun,' Macky said.

'Thanks, Mack. But I need to sit quiet by here now. Those skinheads won't bother us any more.'

Priest was silent. The triumvirate of hard cases downed their brandies and stood up. Sometimes it's like that. You plan a good night out and everything gets sidetracked. What can you do? Anyway, for Macky and Morgan, it was just what a good night out ought to be.

'Well, if you're not coming, fuck it,' said Macky. 'We're off.'

'Hey, thanks, boys,' I said. 'I'll see you next door in an hour or so.'

'I'll stay by here with you,' Priest said.

'Go on up,' I said. 'I got an important phone call to make.'

I winked at him. He nodded. He probably thought that I was going to score.

Macky, Morgan and Gerry swaggered to the door, past caring now about gypsies, coppers, skinheads or any other hostile being that dared to cross their path. Priest's hand shook as he clasped his glass and lifted it to his mouth. He took a swallow, then breathed out hard. There was still a quaver in his voice as he called, 'See you later, Dave.'

'Yeah.'

I was glad to see them go. I was actually going to do it. It was time. I didn't even need the paper in my pocket. I already had her number in my head. And I couldn't put it off any longer. All I needed was a telephone but there wasn't one in the pub. I'd have to go back out on the street. Dodge those skins. Onward and upward, dog brothers. Oh dog sisters, say a little prayer for me.

Chapter 7

1

Wind-whipped, and blustered by a rising storm, I stepped out into the street from the pub doorway. Metamorphosed from inanimate liquid, the beer and brandy in my belly spread from intestine to veins and into the subtle channels of the old sensory system. A warm ball in my belly melted from belly to balls and rolled in a wave to wash through my pumping heart. My face was flushed with blood, each capillary alive and crawling beneath the surface of my skin. Back deep in the skull, the rush of alcohol caused a soft explosion of synaptic fireworks that lit up the world without.

I imagined where I might find a telephone. I searched the street ahead through my memory. Images arose of payphones in pubs I had no wish to enter. The brace on my leg limited the spring in my stride and – like a stiff pole – pivoted me through the fulcrum of my hip, propelling me forward. The thick alcoholic buzz hummed in my inner ear, vibrated throughout my body, and sent me towards the railway station. Although the cold hit me, I felt impervious to it.

The lights were bright on the street. The voices of the few pedestrians echoed in the cavities of my ears and the cars whined by. Mannequins stared out from shop windows, all dead eyes and blank expressions.

There was one face constantly before my mind's living eye, among all those faces who passed me by, testing recognition, and that was Maria Grazia's.

I turned on to Station Road, and cut a sharp diagonal across the deserted street.

The glass entrance of the British Rail ticket office laid a parallelogram of light on the glistening tarmac. I pulled open the tightly sprung doors, a twinge in the injured ribs, and stepped inside. I pressed the silver coins into the hungry slot and punched the numbers that had been running around my head. A thrill fluttered in my belly as the connection was made and I heard the burring tone of the phone ring. Once, twice, three times, four times, a click and then a woman's voice: 'Hello?'

The trapped bird flapped from my belly to my chest.

'Maria Grazia, it's me.'

'Hey, Davey, you called.'

'Yeah, I been out with Morgan and Macky. It's been a bit strange, you know what I mean? I thought I'd get away from them for a while.'

'You want to come over?'

'Hey, that would be nice. I'm just around the corner, I'll be over in a minute, OK?'

'Good. I'll be here.'

'Bye.'

'Bye.'

I hung up.

I came out of the gelid foyer into the street. Still no

sign of the skins. The spring air was turning damper and colder by the minute. My breath hit my upturned leather lapels, moisture condensing on my chin. I already anticipated the glow of her room but I wanted to keep my expectations to a minimum.

The café, above which Maria Grazia lived, was about a hundred yards up the High Street from the station. My mind was beginning to clear of the deepest of the alcoholic fog. The impressions of the street were less kaleidoscopic. The lights and movements of the sparse cars, the noises of the vociferous pedestrians settled into a more stable sensory perception.

There was an ache in my hip. The night's migrations had been long and tiring on my leg. I was ready to rest. The throb of my bruises was making itself felt.

The Queen's Café had been closed all day, Good Friday; the Italians, good Catholics. I rang the doorbell in the recessed entrance. To my left was the big display window full of plates of plaster fried eggs, chips and baked beans, chocolate cakes and coffees, glistening under the street lights, entirely unconvincing.

A light showed in the oblong glass above the door and I heard Maria Grazia's footsteps on the stairs. She opened the door. I loved that tousled mass of hair that fell to the shoulders of her black knitted blouse, the short, tight black skirt that clung to her heavy hips and thighs.

'Hey, come on in, Davey,' she said.

She guided me past her. I could feel her follow me slowly up the stairs to the first-floor flat as I lifted my stiff leg, step by step. The TV was on with the sound turned down. Images of Marlon Brando flickered black and

135

white, reflected in the glass front of the china cabinet. Brando has got a docker's hook. Oldies on the box for the holidays.

I pulled off my leather jacket and Maria Grazia took it. She draped it on a straight-backed chair.

'Sit down, Davey. You look a bit tired, you know.'

I loved those sexy Italian inflections in her Welsh-accented English. I sat on the sofa. A ginger tom came out of the bedroom to investigate the disturbance. The cat leaped into my lap.

'You *are* honoured.' Maria Grazia lit a cigarette. 'Tigre's taken an instant like to you. Do you want a drink, Davey?'

I felt a little wary, given the amount of cider, beer and brandy that I had already consumed.

'Jesus, I don't know. What have you got?'

'How about a little cognac? I am sure you'll like that.'

I nodded. 'Thanks, that's great.'

Maria Grazia got up and walked across the room to a mahogany drinks cabinet. It looked antique. There were a number of bottles of spirits and glasses of every size and shape. The walls were hung with old oil paintings. Family heirlooms. It gave the place a distinctly non-Welsh look. I could never fathom why Maria Grazia's family stayed in the valleys.

She uncorked the cognac bottle. Smoke curled up around the dark ringlets of her hair. She poured the amber liquid into two crystal glasses.

While Maria Grazia was busy with the drinks, I quietly tore open a condom packet and tucked the little pink ring into my shirt pocket. I crumpled the foil and pushed it into the pocket of my jeans. I wondered at my presumption. The alcohol certainly helped. I took care not to disturb the cat who purred, contented, on my knees.

Maria Grazia turned around. She held the faceted bowls. She brought the brandy to the sofa and sat next to me.

'*Salute, carissimo.*' She was smiling.

'Cheers, luv,' I said and clinked my crystal against the clear goblet in Maria Grazia's hand. The cat was affronted by the scent of cognac and twisted from my lap. He flopped on to his side under the coffee table.

I let the cognac vapours be drawn into my nose as I tipped the liquid between my lips. Sweet grape and the melting burn of alcohol in mouth and throat.

'Oh, that's good, Mary Grace.'

'It's my favourite,' she replied. 'A restaurant owner in Italy gave my father a case.'

She let her hand fall on to my knee. I pressed my fingers between hers. She took another sip of cognac and stood up. I savoured the sight of Maria Grazia's plump dark body walking across the room to the drinks cabinet to where her cigarette still burned in the ashtray. The cat leaped up and rubbed against her legs.

My cheeks were red from the heat of the room, the flush of cognac. Maria Grazia turned to face me, the look in her eyes was relaxed, complicit. She blew one more stream of smoke into the air and then ground out her cigarette.

As she sat beside me again, I put down my goblet and tentatively touched her hair. She pressed my hand.

'You're very tender, Davey; not really much like your friends.'

I smiled. 'They're all right. They're just a bit crazy, that's all.'

Maria Grazia curled up beside me. The cat left for the bedroom. She pressed herself closer to me. I didn't have time to register surprise, shyness. Her mouth was open as I kissed her, her breath perfumed with cognac and smoke. I had a moment of panic as the face of Steven Bunyan arose in my mind like Banquo's fucking ghost. Maria Grazia's arms tightened around my body so that her breast, her ribs and her hip pressed into me and I stifled a groan at the sharp stabbing pain that lanced through my ribs. Her tongue was in my mouth, her cheekbones hard on my face, her hair tickling my skin. Fuck the pain. The smell of Maria Grazia was making my head spin. Steven Bunyan had taught me to like the scent of another body. A warmth spread from Maria Grazia's palms on the back of my neck, down through the muscles of my shoulders. Fear, confusion, violence ebbed out. I closed my fingers on her breast. Her hand slid down my thigh and rested between my legs, her breath became a sort of rasp. I nuzzled down under Maria Grazia's jaw to press my lips against her neck. She rubbed her head against mine, right over the swollen egg above my ear. It was all I could do not to wince.

I ran my tongue the length of her neck, buried my nose in her hair. Maria Grazia had both her hands on my face now; her fingers pressed and caressed my cheeks, my nose, my eyes. The pain in my head subsided to a low burn.

'Mmmm . . . I want you,' I whispered.

'I wonder why we whisper when we make love,' she murmured.

Her fingers eased open the buckle of my belt. My hands were under her knitted blouse. I unhooked her brassiere. We were a single tangled animal escaping from the nets of clothing. I wanted to hear her laugh, caress her body, roll with her in that landscape of bed and blanket. She popped the button on my jeans and unzipped me. She rubbed me over my underpants as she kissed me on the lips again. My fingertips traced the patterns of her vertebrae, pressed the soft flesh under her ribs, followed the smooth contours of her hips. Her fingers slipped under my waistband, and she slid down my body. Delicately, she picked a pubic hair off the soft skin near the head of my prick and then bent her head and took me in her mouth. My God, what an analgesic. I let my head fall back against the sofa as Maria Grazia cupped my balls in her hand and bobbed her head slowly. I lay back and relaxed into the warm, wet pleasure.

'Come here, love,' I said.

I pulled her up from my lap so that I could kiss her again. My hand slid under her skirt and I hooked my fingers into her panties. She raised her bottom to let me pull her underwear down. My fingers caressed the curly hairs below Maria Grazia's belly. She pushed her bush against my palm. Her hips rolled forwards and backwards as she pushed herself against my fingers.

'I want you too, Davey,' she whispered.

Maria Grazia broke our embrace. She pulled her

blouse over her head and shrugged off her unfastened bra. I took off my shirt and laid it close by.

'Davey, look at those bruises on your arms and ribs.'

Colourful, they were, and tender.

'It's a long story,' I said. 'I got into a brush today with some skinheads. Macky and Morgan straightened it out, though.'

'You poor boy,' she cooed and her fingers traced the black and blue outlines. Pleasure and pain all in a fingertip. Then her hands were on my thighs again. She unlaced my shoes and pulled up my jeans to unbuckle my leg brace. She opened the velcro wrap and I slid the brace off my skinny, withered leg. She tugged at my jeans. They came off along with my underpants and bared the long red scrape along my other shin.

'Does it hurt?' she asked.

I shook my head.

She made me slide down on to the carpet, lifting my hips. She unfastened her skirt and let it fall to the floor. She kneeled down over me. We kissed and she hung her breasts to brush over my chest. With one hand, I cupped her under her buttocks and pulled her forward. With the other hand, I slipped the condom out from the pocket of my shirt that I had dropped on the carpet, close by. As we kissed, I rolled the rubber on.

Now, I rubbed Maria Grazia's breasts, gently pinched her nipples. I nibbled her ear lobes. She reached down for my cock and her shoulders pulled back. She looked at me in cheery surprise as she touched the protective latex.

140

'We don't need to interrupt anything then, little Davey.'

I wasn't too pleased with the 'little' part but what the fuck. She smiled and she lowered herself on to me till I sank all the way into her. I let out a deep sigh of pleasure. She lifted herself slowly again, and then eased back down, leaned forward again to kiss me. With her on top it was less painful but I wanted her on her back. I locked her in a tight embrace, breathed out against the sharp jab through my ribcage, and we rolled over together so that Maria Grazia was on her back. I let the throbs and aches subside. I brushed my fingertips over her breasts, her ribs, her flanks. Then she started moving again, pushing her hips up, then rolling herself down against my pelvic bone – finding that rhythm together. I squeezed Maria Grazia's breast gently as she began to make little murmurs. Maria Grazia undulated beneath me. We slipped together over the edge into the state where thought fuses out. There were sounds, shudders and a coming to rest. Images continued to flicker – just out of sight – from the silent TV.

It was so surprisingly easy. The first flush of love and its accompanying desire; just beyond that tentative first meeting and the grip of anxiety. Maria Grazia pulled a woollen shawl from the back of the sofa and wrapped it around us. I let myself drift into oblivion.

2

What about that brother of mine, Roger? And what did he have to do with this story anyway? Peripheral perhaps at this point, but essential in the end, as you will see. Perhaps the answer to a prayer. Let us follow him briefly as I floated, semi-conscious, in the arms of Maria Grazia.

He was sitting in the Taj Mahal Indian restaurant with his wife Jill and his mate Ian, the organiser of the Protestant football team, and Ian's wife Annie. It was quiet in the Taj because the pubs were still in full swing. Before eleven o'clock, it was a normal restaurant. After eleven fifteen, it was a potential battle zone. The two married couples sat at a white linen-covered table, as yet unstained, and the proprietor Mohan Singh brought over the menus. They were early-evening regulars here, so Mohan Singh greeted them cordially. Late-evening regulars, he never spoke a word to; generally they were a class of animal beyond the capacity for comprehension of even the simplest English.

'How are you all tonight?' Mohan said.

'Oh, fine, mun,' Roger said. 'How's the wife, Mohan. I heard you were expecting another little one.'

Mohan Singh smiled. 'Oh, she's fine. We're very happy about it. I'm hoping for another strapping great son.'

'There's nice,' Jill said. 'Upstairs now, is it?'

'Indeed,' Mohan said. 'We've got enough people working that she can take it easy. I'd rather have the men here anyway, especially for when the pubs close.'

'Oh, right enough,' said Jill. 'They're bloody mad after a skinful. I don't know how you do it.'

Mohan Singh laughed and moved towards the kitchen.

142

'We'll manage. It is the hardest time of the week though, I'll give you that.'

He disappeared to wherever managers of restaurants manage to disappear to.

'That'll be their third,' Annie said to Jill.

'Prolific bloke, old Mohan,' Roger said. 'Another little brown-skinned Welshman on the way.'

'Well, you need a bitta colour in all this grey and lily-white, innit?' Ian said. 'Hybridisation, son. Make the race stronger. Look at the Yanks. Masters of the world, innit?'

'Oh I draw the line at that,' Jill said.

'Yeah, but you wouldn't even marry a bloody Protestant, would you?' Roger said.

'I married you, and your religion's football,' she said.

Well, they had a leisurely curry and left the restaurant. Down the street from where they'd parked the car was a big crowd of skinheads between the Castle Cinema and the old town hall. Jill took the wheel of the Chevette. She backed the car into the alley by the restaurant so that she wouldn't have to go in the direction of the noisy mob who were already too close for comfort.

'Pass up by the Blaen View,' Roger said. 'We'll call in after and see if the old man wants a lift.'

Jill turned left below the cenotaph and right on to the Brecon Road. She approached the corner where the pub stood. Dai Ryan, the barman, was on the pavement outside, sweeping up glass and rubbish. Jill slowed the car down.

'Hey, look,' Roger said. 'There's my old man and

143

Johnny Rees coming out of the priests' house. Pull over, Jill.'

Ben closed the great iron gate behind him and then him and Johnny Rees crossed the street towards the car. Ben had a look of relief on his face. Roger got out.

'Dad, we're just taking Ian and Annie home now. Wait in the Blaen View and we'll come and pick you up then.'

'Thanks, son,' Ben said, 'Can you give Johnny a lift home, too?'

'Well aye, mun. What happened b'there then, Dad?'

'Some bloody yobs broke the window. The police got one of them. They had him for stabbing one of the boys from the bar. One of them skinheads.'

'Oh, bloody madness it is,' Jill said.

'Go in b'there now, Dad, and we'll be up in a minute,' Roger said.

He got back in the car.

'Skinheads,' Ian said. 'Not a clue, mun. Mad as bloody hatters.'

They dropped off Ian and Annie down the street, right outside the door of their terraced house.

'See you tomorrow, Ian. I'll get them home.'

Jill drove back to the pub as quickly as she could. Ben and Johnny Rees were standing in the doorway waiting for them. They rode in silence through the dark streets. They dropped Johnny at his door and made their way to Maeve and Ben's house.

'Come in and have a cup of tea,' Ben said.

'All right then,' Jill said.

They sat in the front room in an awkward silence. Something had disturbed Ben, and Roger put it down to the skinheads. Maeve made them all a cup of tea and a few rounds of ham sandwiches. Ben had repeated the story of the incidents at the Blaen View for them but he didn't mention his visit to the rectory. Roger and Jill were so taken up by the skinhead and stabbing story that they didn't even think about asking Ben why he'd been coming out of the priests' house.

Maeve was visibly upset, pulling at her blue-rinsed hair, shifting her pinny at neck and waist.

'I saw them, see, on their way down town,' she said. 'They were throwing ashcans on the street up here, right outside our door. There's a terrible mess out there. I was afraid to death that they'd start causing some real damage to the cars or somebody's house, but they hadn't worked themselves up enough for that yet, I suppose. They should lock the bloody lot of them up; and give them the birch. The birch would make them think twice, I can tell you.'

'Nothing makes them think twice, Mam,' put in Roger. 'When they put some of them inside they feel better off in there than they do out here, so I don't know what there is to do about it.'

'If they had a good ten strokes of the birch on their backs, like they used to do, they'd never forget it,' Maeve said.

'It's terrible,' Ben said. 'It's gone beyond. Used to be that if you stayed away from certain pubs, you never had to worry. The fighters knew where to go if they wanted to fight, and decent people stayed in their own pubs. Now, you can't feel safe even in your own home.'

'It's the quality of life has gone down,' said Jill. 'It's getting worse every day. Nobody believes in anything any more, that's the trouble. Everybody is out for number one and they don't care at all about anyone else and it starts at the bloody top with the government. It's all over the TV, innit? Look out for number one. If people don't start to look out for one another soon, it's only going to get worse. It'll be dog eat dog on the streets, and we'll have muggings and burglaries and murders and riots the like of which we can't even imagine now. Worse it'll get, nothing else.'

'It'll be bad down there tonight, anyway,' Roger said.

'Why don't you go down in the car, Rog, and see if you can find your brother?' Maeve said. 'Get him up out of there while these bloody lunatics are about. Jill can stay up here and wait for you.'

Roger shifted on the settee, uncomfortable in his skin.

'I can't do that, Mam. I've had a few pints and I'm over the limit if they stop me. I'll tell you what though, Jill can drive us home and I'll stop by the Gynlais to see if I can find him. I'll ask him if he wants a lift to his flat, or to stay up our house. You know what he is though. He's a stubborn bugger. I'll phone to tell you if I see him.'

'You're the only one he talks to, Rog, you know that,' said Ben. (Ben had always kept up the pretence to Maeve that he never spoke to me either.)

'I'll make us another cup of tea,' said Maeve.

Roger and Jill got up to go.

'I'll call you in about an hour,' Roger said.

Ben and Maeve sat in their armchairs, silent. Their

eyes were fixed on the TV screen. Eamonn Andrews greeted an overdressed American comedienne with a fondness for plastic surgery. The studio audience applauded and the brassy orchestra played a vaudeville tune. Ben and Maeve's attention was fixed on the telephone behind them, though they never looked once in that direction.

3

When I came round again, Maria Grazia was up and had switched off the TV. She had her clothes in her arms and she motioned me to follow her into the bathroom. I picked up my clothes and the brace and sort of hopped after her.

'Oh, I'm sorry,' she said.

I waved it off and leaned against the door jamb. I mean, I felt fucking great.

The paint was a little flaked off the wall from the moisture but I was really amazed to see that the walls had been painted with pillars and clouds and those angels you see floating at absurd angles inside the rooms of castles. I mean, this was her flat.

'Who did these pictures then?' I said.

She turned on the shower and steam began to rise. It rolled out of the bathtub and floated close to the clouds that decorated the walls and ceilings.

'I did,' she said.

She stepped under the shower and pulled the curtain just halfway across. Not to seem like she was cutting me off, I thought. I had to struggle to get in the tub because my bad leg didn't have the support of the brace. It was much easier than I thought it would be.

'I didn't know you were such a good painter,' I said.

Maria Grazia turned under the hot spray.

'You don't know much about me at all yet, except you like to fuck me.'

I felt a bit taken aback at that somewhat stunning but really irrefutable statement. She let me get under the hot water. I had to say something.

'Well, look, I don't know what else is going on here but I do know it's more than what our bodies just did.'

Hollow, I thought, but she didn't seem to mind.

She pulled me towards her and I rubbed soap across her back and her sides, making her fleshy rolls slippery. She leaned back from me so that I could soap her breasts and belly and then pressed herself against my skin. I began to get horny again. She took the soap from my hands and began to wash me, carefully around and over the bruises.

'Painting is my passion,' she said and she stood away from me to let the shower rinse me off. The heat was easing the pain away. 'You must come with me to Italy some time. Almost every little church there has a masterpiece.'

She was careful not to get her hair wet. I tried hard to keep my balance and wash my armpits.

'I wish I had some clean clothes to put on after this shower,' I said.

'I'll lend you a T-shirt and some socks,' she offered. She shut off the shower. We got out of the tub

– she graceful, me awkward – and she handed me a towel.

'Come on,' she said, 'let me show you something.'

She led me – limping badly, brace in hand – down the hall to her bedroom. The four walls and the ceiling were all painted with more scenes out of Paradise. There were trees, with these goat-legged people running around them and women falling out of wispy tunics. There were broken pillars. The ceiling had bright light that shone out from between white clouds and trumpet-blowing cherubs floated in the four directions. You could only get away with that in Italy, I thought, but there it was in Merthyr. Stunning. Heavy blue velvet curtains – open – framed the bay window. Outside, the darkness of the night was lit up by the yellow of a street light. The window looked like a doorway into another world – a world that we were inevitably going to re-enter, the world of skinheads and beer and acid and speed, and gypsies and perverts and sundry hard cases.

Maria Grazia tossed me a white T-shirt, some striped socks and a pair of plain white cotton knickers. At least I could feel clean under my day-old clothes. I started getting dressed while Maria Grazia slid open the painted doors of her wardrobe and chose a black skirt and top. I saw that there were large books on the top shelf of the closet. I was buckling up the brace when she tossed a heavy volume on to the bed. It sank into the soft coverlet. Maria Grazia began to pull on her pantyhose. I got my jeans back on and then started to flip through the pages of the book on the bed: *Art Treasures of the Vatican*. What the fuck was this all about? Was she trying to tell me she was a good little Catholic girl?

'Look at this,' I said. 'Here's one of those popes on a throne and there's all these half-naked women all around him, titties everywhere.'

'That's a Botticelli mural,' she said.

I was fascinated. I turned the pages slowly while Maria Grazia pulled at the thighs of her pantyhose to get them in place. Behind her, on the wall, a satyr was trying to plant a kiss on a nymph. She took out a pair of black court shoes from the bottom of the wardrobe. I flipped open the next section of the book. There was a sideways, two-page spread of *The Last Judgement* by Michelangelo. Maria Grazia draped her arm around my shoulders. I enjoyed the feel of her breast against my arm, the smell of her hair.

'Michelangelo,' she said, 'all his life, he struggled with the conflict between his passion and his spirituality. Look here, you see, these are his political opponents in the Vatican falling into Hell. You know what's funny. He didn't know where to put himself – lifted up to salvation, or tumbling into damnation.'

I was getting lessons in art and history from this beautiful woman that I'd just made love with. It was like Heaven had just materialised on Earth.

'Let's go this summer,' I said. 'Down to Italy, I mean. We'll get into all that vino, and spaghetti, and lovemaking, and paintings and ruins. I'd love that.'

She laughed and said, 'I want to go out for a while. I feel I've missed all the party.'

Party? I thought. Fucking hell, what a party!

'Let's go out and join those friends of yours,' she

said, 'They're probably sitting in the Taj Mahal by
now, if they're following their unbreakable Friday-
night rituals.'

I felt on top of the world. I didn't exactly get to
discuss Botticelli and Michelangelo with Morgan and
Macky very often. Perhaps we could start tonight over
a bucket of vindaloo.

4

The kitchen was in a controlled frenzy. Mohan Singh
kept a stern eye on the plate-juggling waiters and
the tandoori chefs. Of course, the big vats of rogan
josh, chicken korma, meat madras and meat vindaloo
bubbled on the industrial range; the dishes had been
prepared earlier in the day for the onslaught that always
came when the pubs closed.

As a restaurant manager of quality, Mohan Singh
was certainly more comfortable with the steady flow
of diners from six o'clock until ten. After that, the
well-dressed and sober couples left for home and there
was a lull in the culinary proceedings. That was the
time when the restaurant staff braced themselves for
pub-closing time. The only thing that Mohan Singh
could say for the hours between eleven and one in
the morning was that he made a lot of money from
drunks. During these last hours, the restaurant turned
into a room full of hungry animals, some cheered
and some embittered by drink. Mohan Singh kept a
bouncer on the door to ensure that the worst of the
troublemakers were kept out but there were never

any guarantees. He often wondered if it was worth his while to have himself and his waiters undergo the racist slurs and threats of violence that his patrons felt free to offer when their inhibitions had been dissolved in alcohol. Mohan Singh, however, was a shrewd businessman. The fact was that he made more money in the two two-hour periods on Friday and Saturday night than he did on lunch and dinner from Monday to Thursday. It did nothing, of course, to engender in him any optimism for the future of race relations in the country in which he had chosen to make his home.

Apart from the overt racism of the drunks, he also had to deal with the public health inspectors. Every restaurant owner had to deal with the peculiarities of perishables, and the voracity of creatures from bacteria to rodents who sought to assault the kitchen: a paradise of comestible abundance. Mohan acknowledged the fact that the previous Indian restaurant in town had been closed down for having deceased domestic animals found in the food preparation area. (No doubt, he thought, a form of revenge on particularly obnoxious patrons.) Mohan felt it was an insult to him that the public health inspectors visited so regularly, with an air that suggested that the restaurant staff were trying to hide some crime of Sweeney Todd-like proportions, or rampant risk of disease.

Mohan Singh had an overwhelming pride in the culinary traditions of his forebears. He longed to replicate regal Mughal delicacies to educate the palates of the generally undiscerning British public. It was an attitude that would perhaps have had more success in a larger urban centre such as Cardiff, or Swansea, or Bristol for that matter. His cousin had persuaded him to come to the valleys. Amrit Singh owned an electrical appliance shop in this town. It was Amrit who had told him of the opportunity when the previous Indian restaurant had been closed down. 'It is a monopoly business,' he'd said. He had convinced Mohan that all these people needed was to experience an Indian restaurant of quality. 'Word will spread to towns around, and that will bring people flocking in. That is what happened with my Amrit's Discount Stereo Centre for superior goods at knockdown prices.'

Unfortunately, it was easier for the valleys' dwellers to relate to consumer electrical equipment than to the subtleties of delicate combinations of spices. The pub-closing crowd wanted something hot and meaty. Their taste buds had long been numbed by strong drink. He checked his watch. It said ten to eleven.

Chapter 8

1

Low lamps half lit the room as if the red velvet wallpaper could suck light out of the air. At every table, drunks of every description hunched over plates of unknown brown sauces and plates of rice and soggy chips arranged upon the stained, once-white linens. Macky, Morgan, Gerry and Priest were already in the curry house when me and Maria Grazia arrived. I was as high as a fucking kite after sex with Maria Grazia, albeit encumbered by the old creaking brace which now seemed to want to launch me towards the stippled ceiling. I was beaming, a moon in that thick aromatic atmosphere. Maria Grazia was stunning, though you might not have known it by the lack of reaction in that room full of obsessive piggery.

Macky waved us over, twinkles in the deep-sunk eyes, the little cherub lips slightly pursed over his broken teeth. The affable Morgan screwed up his face and the scar on his forehead was like a red headlamp. His big-fingered hand waved at the two empty chairs kept for us at the table. How come they had two, I have no idea, since they were only expecting me.

'You two been busy,' Macky said.

Priest began strangling a napkin, giving us both knowing nods.

'Well, we're here now, innit?' I said.

'I'm hungry,' Maria Grazia said.

There was something edgy about Macky. He kept glancing at the door and fidgeting on his seat as if he really wanted to be somewhere else. He pulled at his curly hair, then jerked his head up like a speed-freak on a bad comedown. It made me nervous.

'You don't look so fucking hot, Mack,' I said. 'What's up?'

'Macky's still worried about his dog, Spaz,' Morgan said. He turned towards Macky. 'You're lucky that dog didn't come wandering round the alley by this place, Mack, or you might find him in a nice biriani.'

Macky looked across at him. 'Fuck this,' he said. 'I've got to go up and see if he's all right. It's been bugging me all night, mun.'

Morgan shook his head in exasperation. 'Well, you'll have to wait a bit for a taxi, Mack, because they'll all be out taking the pub boys home by now.'

'Don't matter about a taxi,' said Macky. 'I'll get the Kwaka and ride up.'

'What fucking Kwaka?' Gerry said.

'The Kawasaki they put me inside for, but never found,' Macky said.

Morgan peered at him with that narrow-eyed expression of his that he got when he was suspicious. Macky had a big fucking grin on his face all of a sudden.

'Where is it then?' I said.

'It's up in Kenny's garage, Spaz. I told him to hide it till I came out; and to keep it in good running order too. That's what a mechanic's for, innit?'

'You'll have every fucking copper in town after you if they see you on that,' Gerry said. 'Stay by here now, and have a curry.'

We all knew that if Macky had decided to do anything, there wasn't much hope of dissuading him. Maria Grazia wasn't that clued in, so she gave it a try.

'Macky, you know how many police vans are out at closing time. They're bound to see you.'

She reached across the table and put her hand on Macky's scabbed and tattooed fingers. I didn't like that.

'Please, stay with us and have something to eat,' she said.

Macky just laughed, then he held up her fingers and touched them to his lips. I didn't like that either. He smiled that broken-toothed smile of his.

'I have never given a fuck about coppers in my life,' he said. 'And I fancy a ride on the Kawasaki, so I better call Ken, like.'

At the prospect of riding the bike again, he was suddenly beaming from ear to ear. He got up from the table and went towards the public telephones that were next to the main entrance. At that moment, a drunken Steven Bunyan, like the fucking shadow of my bad luck, walked into the restaurant alone. He swayed across the room and Macky almost decked him as he went past. Pity he didn't. Then the Indian waiter showed up to take our orders and blocked the ugly bastard from sight. I was glad. I opened the menu without really looking at what was there. Gerry ordered poppadoms and parathas and then he was interrupted by requests for vindaloos, chicken madrases and sag joshes, rice, raita and nan, from Priest, Morgan and Maria Grazia.

'I'll have a bhuna josh,' I said, more to say something than anything else.

Bunyan, the reeling, reeking drunk, made a bee-line for our table. Without so much as a greeting, he began to paw at Maria Grazia's arm and fawn over her shoulder. I got up slowly to punch the bastard out but Maria Grazia was between me and him.

'Oh, you're so beautiful,' he burbled.

She slapped his hands away. 'What the hell you think you doing?'

Bunyan swayed back and I lunged for the cunt. Priest grabbed me from behind.

'Hold on, Dave, or the bouncer'll be here.'

'Sit down, now, butty,' I said to Bunyan. 'Or I'll fucking break you.'

I could too, leg or no fucking leg. Bunyan swayed and started to say something but seemed to forget what it was. He staggered towards an empty table near the wall. The bouncer by the door was already gliding across the room between the tables. He grabbed Bunyan by the shoulder and pushed him down into a seat. He obviously knew who he was talking to.

'Listen, Bunyan, my boy,' he said. 'You sit there now and I'll have them bring you a nice chicken korma like you always have. But if you get up, even to go to the lav, I will personally escort you to the alley round the back and break your fucking legs.'

I wished that he had just taken him out and done it. If I did anything now the bouncer would be all over me. I might be able to give Bunyan a pounding but not the bouncer. Bunyan sat down where the bouncer had showed him. He nodded blearily, put his elbows on his table and his hands on his forehead.

'Sorry, mate; sorry, love,' the bouncer said to me and Maria Grazia. 'He'll be all right now. You know how it is, like. He won't give you any more trouble.'

I raised my hands, palms out, and nodded to the bouncer. 'Thanks, mate. OK,' I said.

It was better to sit down and ignore it.

'What a fucking prick,' Morgan said.

Gerry just nodded. Maria Grazia twined her fingers in mine. I still felt pissed off at her for grabbing Macky's hand, never mind that cunt Bunyan. Bunyan was a bad memory, my worst memory, and bad fucking luck, I thought, to boot.

'Everything OK?' Priest asked.

Gerry and Morgan shrugged. Those dark eyes of Maria Grazia looked into mine. She was obviously shaken. Her fingers were cold. How could you stay pissed off at that fucking vision of total sex and love? I put my arm around her. I glanced back. Bunyan seemed close to nodding off in his seat.

'Take it easy, Dave. OK?' said Priest.

'Yeah. All right,' I said.

It wasn't often I got a chance to play the hard boy.

Macky sauntered back from the public telephone. He had missed the altercation completely. He was jubilant.

'I'll be up and back in a minute now, boys. Order something for Kenny. I offered to take him home on the bike but he don't want to be seen on it with me. Afraid they'll have him for aiding and abetting.'

The food started to arrive then and took over the attention of all of them, except me and Maria Grazia. We picked at small tastes of curry with our forks while the four others dug into their dishes and mopped at sauces with flapping parathas and hot slabs of nan.

'Eat up over there,' Priest said to me.

I couldn't help but smile at him. He had forgotten all about his barney with Macky. And just then Kenny the mechanic walked in. He kept his helmet on.

'Kenny, have a bite, son!' Macky shouted.

Kenny's eyes shifted under the visor. A muffled voice came out. 'Here's the fucking keys. I'm off out of it, Mack. Patsy followed me down in the van to give me a ride home.'

'Fucking great, Ken,' Macky said.

And Kenny, still in the helmet, turned and disappeared out the door.

Macky dropped a five-pound note on to the table. 'That ought to cover mine, boys. I'll see you in half an hour, or more, or tomorrow, or whatever.'

Morgan waved a fork, Gerry grunted.

'Watch out, Mack,' I said. 'For fuck's sake.'

Maria Grazia squeezed my thigh under the table. I got a hard-on like the fucking bars on the brace. Macky was off now. What could you do but wish him well, good luck, all that shit? At the table, the curry was rapidly disappearing. Macky waved back from the door. He was eager for speed, I could see. I squeezed Maria's fingers, picked up a fork in my left hand and prodded at the meat in the curry as Macky disappeared through the door.

2

You need to know what happened to Macky. I need to tell it too. In the best way I can. The story came out piece by bloody piece like picking shattered bone from an uncooked and badly butchered lamb chop. I got a lot of it from Clara, the gypsy girl, and she was there for the worst of it. I was there for a lot of it myself, as you'll see. If the rest is the result of my fevered imagination, it's because he was my fucking mate and I need to tell it right. One good thing about being a cripple, when you want something so badly and you can't have it, you can imagine what it's like in every precise fucking detail. I have never sat in the saddle of a 750cc motorbike, the withered foot could never change the gears, but by Christ, I've ached to do it. Here in my chronicle, I will tell how Macky took off on that epic ride into legend.

3

The Kawasaki started first time. Macky could hardly contain himself. He was a cocktail of booze, adrenalin and insane fear for the welfare of his dog. He kicked the bike into gear and whipped back the throttle. A throaty roar echoed down the high street. The machine bulleted forward, clutched in Macky's fanatic grip. Perfect.

The street flashed by. No cars anywhere, and no police vans.

There were no people.

He gunned the bike. The red brick of the General Hospital disappeared behind him. The High Street curved out of town and Macky pulled off the main drag on to the rise of a side road. Above him, hairpin bends hung on the remains of the iron slag mountain known as the Whitey. He rose on the lower slopes of that unnatural plateau which bore the scars of blasting. Crushing machines had carved into the slopes. Conveyor belts girdled the piles of hardcore that were ready to be hauled away.

He left behind the last street light on the road. The bright beam of the Kawasaki cut a rapid path through the night's blackness. Macky banked the bike around each curve, his knee inches from the tarmac that snaked beneath him. He was close to home now. His two-roomed shack was perched on the hillside close to a shale outcrop. It had been built by some coal picker in the Great Depression, and then abandoned. When Macky had found it, he had thrown out years of rotting debris and made the place liveable. There was new corrugated iron on the roof. He had dragged in a few pieces of second-hand furniture. There was a shotgun padlocked in the cupboard and a few cans of food stacked in a wooden orange crate for emergencies.

The Kwaka rounded the final bend and Macky hit the brakes. He was still fifty yards away, and he saw that a campfire was burning on the open ground about ten yards from his front door. He brought the bike to a skidding halt, spraying gravel in a wide arc around him.

Cigarette tips glowed in the darkness, flat-capped shadows flitted across the lit-up wall of his house. Macky could hear laughter: high peals of the women; that of the men like gruff barks. He coasted to a stop in front of the fire, letting the engine idle. The gypsies from the Welly were there, one with his nose taped up – a hospital job, no doubt. Sitting on stones next to the fire were the three gypsy girls that he and Morgan had tripped with. Including the one called Clara that he had got into bed. She wouldn't look at him, but poked at the fire with a small stick. A long piece of meat turned on a wooden spit.

'You like a bite to eat, Mack?'

It was the fat one who spoke, Bridey by name, short of breath, malicious and unforgiving.

'I told you, I'd never refuse anything from a woman.'

Macky looked at the quiet one, Clara. She stayed with her head down, her face lit up by the fire. Bridey picked up a long kitchen knife. She began to carve slices of meat from the skinny leg on the spit, catching each piece on a plate that she had taken from Macky's kitchen.

162

'Here you are, Macky,' she said, and lifted the plate in a gesture of offering.

Macky wasn't about to get off the Kawasaki. He looked around to see if anyone had his shotgun. Most of the men cupped cigarettes in the curve of their fingers, or kept their hands in their pockets. Their faces were silent, shadowed – ugly in the firelight.

'Bring it over here, love,' Macky said. 'I might not be staying long.'

Bridey struggled to her feet and walked around the fire. The men closed behind her in a line, but stopped when Macky gunned the Kwaka's engine. The fat woman handed him the plate, satisfied.

Macky kept looking at the men as he picked up a bit of meat and put it in his mouth. The flesh was a little dry and stringy, but not unpleasant.

'You killed my fucking dog, didn't you?' he said, deliberately putting another piece of meat in his mouth.

'Didn't need to, Mack.'

A nasal whine came from the gypsy with the taped face. One of the younger men shone a powerful flashlight towards a pole in the garden, from which was strung a line to the house. The melted remains of a metal pulley were fused to the line. The long cable lead was still attached to the dog's neck. Its hair was scorched and still stood on end, the rictus lips pulled back from the teeth.

'The lightning done it, Mack,' the nasal voice said.

Macky saw that the dog's hindquarters were missing, and his eyes flicked back to the fire and the spit, and then to the gypsy girl's face. That old acid trip. The words of prophecy. Macky handed the plate back to the girl. A burning hate pumped through his body. Flame red. Faces red, everything red. There was a click as he hit the gear and a roar as he let out the clutch and jerked the throttle. The Kwaka bucked forward. Front wheel high, man and machine hurtled at the taped-faced figure. The gypsy took the tyre full in the chest and was ploughed backwards through flames, embers and roasting meat.

Macky wrenched the handlebars around to regain control of the bike, and whiplashed the back end so that he pointed towards the road again. Knives flashed orange from the flames. There was the pop and tinkle of bottles being shattered against stone. The men closed around him to cut off his escape but the Kwaka lurched forward and Macky crashed into a gauntlet of slashing stabbing hands. He felt steel and glass tear at the flesh of his arms and his chest and the sucking puncture of a knife blade that penetrated his side somewhere under his ribs.

Macky fought to hold the Kwaka under control, as blood wetted the thighs of his jeans. He'd been right about the dog. He felt like throwing up. He wondered how he was going to get somewhere to stop the bleeding. The cuts didn't bother him so much but that hole in his side he knew was serious. Those gyppos might trash his shack. But, then again, probably not. They'd done what they had come for. The scales of cosmic justice were balanced again.

Macky needed help. He wanted to get bandaged up, a pad to staunch the bleeding. If this was a hospital job, someone had to take care of the Kwaka. He marvelled at how clear-headed you could be when you needed to be.

He could hear the red ocean in the convolutions of the shell of his ear. He could hear a full-blown band, a skirling like uillean pipes, the sucking in his guts like the bagpipe's bellows. He was roaring down the road towards the remnants of the Whitey. Dragonlike, the maws of cranes hung over the hillsides. The dead conveyor belts on spindle legs lay silent in the darkness. The bodhrán beat of his blood pulsed and throbbed in the cavity of his skull. Ebb tide. The motorbike bucked beneath him as he hit the bumps and potholes in the road, not caring now to avoid them. He always had loved the feel of the wind that whipped against his face, whistling and wailing like a banshee as it slipped past his speeding form. He was among the bright lights now, the Doppler effect of yells echoing in his ears as he rode back into town and on down High Street.

Chapter 9

1

In town, Bugsy was tamping. Around him, the Shop Boys, the Bus Boys and the Pentrebach Boys were all at maximum, ready for some really heavy aggro. They were bottled into a section of the High Street where the tarmac had been torn up to do some pipe work. The trench was covered with a steel plate, and trestle signs and orange tape were set up around it. The crowd of skins was all squeezed together between the roadworks paraphernalia and Manette's Clothes Shop. No sign of Morgan and Macky on the High Street, which was good for Bugsy. No one in his right mind would go up against those boys. Even if you were sent down for a couple of months, no matter how miserable the bird you would have to do, that was it – over with. But with Morgan and Macky, you wouldn't be safe for the rest of your life. All the skins knew it. And there was plenty to do in town without committing suicide. The coppers seemed to have deserted the streets. People on the high street dived into the nearest pub when they saw them coming. It was too easy.

'It's a skinhead dictatorship, boys!' Bugsy yelled and everybody cheered.

'We are the champions! We are the champions!'

'It's all ours!' shouted Bugsy. 'Let's get what belongs to us.'

The boys looked puzzled. Well, he'd show them what he meant. Bugsy grabbed a red-and-white road-works sign, swung round in a full circle with this big triangular discus and flung it full-force at the window of Amrit's Discount Stereo Centre. The plate glass shattered in a musical avalanche, shards cascading over the pavement. Bugsy kicked in the jagged teeth at the bottom of the window frame. He started handing out cassette players and VCRs to his Firm.

'I'm the fucking boy here! I'm the fucking boy!' he yelled.

He jerked his thumb at his chest. Hands grabbed for the booty. Heads swivelled around to see if anyone was watching. The burglar alarm wailed. Then they all heard a siren and saw the flashing blue lights.

A van and two panda cars stopped about fifty yards away. First tactical mistake by the coppers. About ten of them jumped from the van and the cars and they stood in a thin blue line. They drew their truncheons but in front of the pumped-up crowd of skins the coppers looked strangely vulnerable. None of them was wearing riot gear. One of the Pentrebach Boys picked up a heavy round stone from the pile of dirt beside the trench and hurled it with all his strength towards the advancing blue line. The rock bounced ten feet in front of the coppers who quickened their pace forward. The Pentrebach Boys grabbed at rocks and pieces of broken paving stone from around the hole and began hurling them at the charging Old Bill. A rain of tarmac, concrete and stones ripped into the ten coppers. Two of them went down, one with a head wound, another clutching his knee. Their mates around them were stunned. Four of them grabbed the injured and they all ran back to the van and panda cars. The hail of debris clattered on to the vehicles, but the skinheads stayed close to the handy pile of rubble, and to the rapidly diminishing supplies of electrical goods that Ianto and his brother were still passing out of the appliance shop.

One of the coppers shouted into a panda's radio mike to get reinforcements. The van started up, made a three-point turn and drove off to take the injured cops to hospital. Five or six uniforms still hung back with the pandas. Behind the skins, a hundred yards back up the street, taxis began to arrive in town again to pick up the restaurant trade. Seeing the ruckus down the road, a couple of drivers got out of their cars to watch the action. Bugsy knew he had to get rid of the coppers.

'Drive those bastards out of here!' Bugsy yelled. He picked up an armful of rocks and ran towards the remaining coppers, chucking stone after stone through the air. They hit windscreens, bonnets, the road. The other skins joined in and another hail of rocks crashed on to the metal and glass of the panda cars. The drivers got the pandas in reverse and screamed down the street. The coppers left on foot broke into a panicked run down the high street and the skins howled with the joy of it.

'Hold up! Hold up!'

Bugsy stopped the rush.

'What's next, Bugsy?' Lenny shouted.

Bugsy looked around at the high street shops. He had

to work fast. He knew that the coppers weren't going to try and come at them again till the force had regrouped, but they would definitely be back pretty quick. Bugsy clocked the clothes shops, a fishmonger's, a jeweller's with heavy shutters over the windows. Nothing worth the bother. He looked up the street. The bright electric sign of the Taj Mahal curry house jutted above the high street, with its white neon light in a stylised outline of the marble mausoleum. It blazed like a beacon in the crystal-clear night.

'Fucking nignogs!' Bugsy screamed. 'Let's get 'em!' and he jabbed his finger at the restaurant sign up the street.

'Wogs out! Wogs out! Wogs out!'

The skins were screaming and grabbing handfuls of rocks, dirt, paving stones and cracked tarmac. They charged up the street towards the restaurant. The first rain of stones made the watching taxi drivers break and run, abandoning their cars as the wave of skins surged towards them. Bugsy had never gone off as good as this before. Even when he had been with the Ninian Park Boys and smashed all the windows in the street leading to Bristol Rovers football ground. Even when he had helped beat ten of their supporters to a miserable pulp and had sent them all to hospital. Better than the fight with the Liverpool fans that he had been in with his pal Gripper. He had taken Gripper's place. They were his boys, not Gripper's, who had driven off the coppers, and now Bugsy wanted to cap it by wiping that restaurant full of Pakis right off the fucking map. He was screaming and banging into the skins all around him. Exploding in ecstatic rage, he was slam-dancing in the streets. He grabbed a triangular piece of paving stone, a good foot long, raised it above his head, and hurled it at the restaurant window with all his might. The stone seemed to arch in slow motion. He saw it as if each frame of a film was flickering as he followed the looped trajectory towards the plate glass painted with a picture of the Taj Mahal and its lake under a night sky filled with splotchy stars and a full moon. The rock hit and the picture exploded into a thousand fragments. A cascade of dirt and rocks followed the paving stone into the restaurant. Bugsy heard the screams of the women and the shouts of the men inside.

2

One of the screaming women was Maria Grazia and some of the shouting was me and Priest and Morgan and Gerry. Tables had been overturned. Glass, curry, rice, blood and stones were all over the dark carpet. Customers and waiters were falling over each other trying to escape through the fire exit at the back of the restaurant. Gashed heads, torn clothes, a cacophony of cooks and crashing utensils. The skins charged the restaurant, coming in through the empty window frame. Bugsy stood there admiring the mess in the front half of the dining room. Then he looked shocked when he saw Morgan and Gerry standing at that point in the room where the debris of the frontal assault had reached its limit. Then there was me and Maria Grazia and Priest behind them, scared shitless, but Morgan and Gerry looked anything but. Most of the crowd was still chanting outside. But the skins in the restaurant knew the two men in front of them.

'O'right, Bugs?' Morgan said.

Bugsy nodded.

'We're going out the back way,' Morgan said.

Bugsy nodded again.

I put my arm around Maria Grazia. She seemed so round and fleshy and soft.

'Oh my God, Davey,' she said. 'What are we going to do?'

There wasn't a lot we could do.

'Fuck off out of it,' I said.

I squeezed her arm and, limping, guided her after Morgan, Gerry and Priest towards the kitchen. It was fucking chaos in there. Hot chaos. Vats of steaming curry boiled on the burners. The other customers and waiters had already gone but six skinheads had already forced their way into the kitchen by the side door. Four of them stood there and launched pots and plates into the alley where the restaurant staff were. I recognised Ianto, one of the Shop Boys, who was smashing the plates in the sink. Another skin had found a cleaver and was chopping at the cutting boards and countertops.

'Turn that stinking curry off,' screeched Ianto.

The Cleaver Kid swung around and smashed the blade clean through the copper pipe at the side of the stove. The flames beneath the pots went dead.

'Let us through!' Gerry shouted.

Cleaver Kid spun to face Gerry, realised who it was, tossed the cleaver away and put his hands up. Boys at the door turned to see Morgan and Gerry and cleared a way to the door for us. It was cooler in the dark alley. The

171

cooks and waiters were sheltering under the wooden stairway that led to the flat above the restaurant. Most of them had knives or cleavers. Mohan Singh looked sick to the stomach.

'Where are the damn police?' he yelled from behind the wall of his staff.

'Davey, these skinheads will kill them,' Maria Grazia said.

What the fuck could *I* do? The waiters were well armed and definitely well motivated and the cops were bound to arrive any second.

Mrs Singh appeared in the doorway of the flat.

'Get the children,' shouted Mohan Singh. 'We have to get you out of here.'

Mrs Singh turned back into the flat and Mohan rushed up the steps to help his wife.

'It's Mrs Singh,' Maria Grazia said. 'We've got to help them.'

I definitely wanted to help against those racist bastards but we were caught between the skins and the Indians and I wanted Maria Grazia out of there as much as I wanted out myself. Morgan, Gerry and Priest were at the end of the alley close to the high street.

'Let's go,' Priest yelled at us.

Mohan Singh appeared on the balcony and came down the stairs, the two-year-old in his arms. The older boy was in his wife's arms.

'Mohan, the whole night's takings are in the restaurant. We can't lose all that,' screamed Mrs Singh.

'Lakshmi, please, it's already gone!' yelled Mohan.

A phalanx of armed cooks and waiters closed around their boss, his wife and their children.

'Come on, they've got it under control,' I said.

Morgan, Gerry and Priest were back on the High Street and me and Maria Grazia arrived behind them.

'Coppers! Fucking loads of them!'

I recognised Bugsy's voice.

Now at the end of the alley, the waiters cheered as they saw the skinheads run, only a few turning to hurl a rock at the cops. Now we were outside the restaurant, and between the skinheads and the cops. More skins tumbled out of the restaurant through the broken window and the front door.

'Bugsy's got a Molotov!' screamed one of the girls.

It was true. Bugsy was out in the middle of the street. He looked bigger than life somehow. Alone. He held the bottle in his hands, staring hard down the street at the advancing line of policemen. He flicked on his cigarette lighter.

'Oh Jesus,' I said.

I pulled Maria Grazia down between two abandoned taxis. A group of SPG in riot gear, advancing up the street, stopped when they saw the rag take light. Then Bugsy spun around and tossed the flaming bottle into the wreckage of the restaurant. A ball of orange light and heat exploded inside the window.

'Fuck you all!' Bugsy yelled.

'Oh Davey, it'll burn to the ground,' Maria Grazia said.

'That's it. End of story,' I said. 'Get the fuck outta here.'

We were out in the middle of the street behind a line of broken and abandoned taxi cars. The five of us drifted down towards the cops as rocks fell all around us. The waiters, Mohan and his wife and kids came out of the alley where they could see the flames and smoke tumbling from the ruined window.

'Oh my restaurant!' Mohan screamed.

Mrs Singh was crying, the children wailing, the waiters yelling. Most of the skins were in full flight but a few more rocks bounced around us and off the perspex shields of the SPG.

'Fuck! The gas!' I shouted. 'In the kitchen! Mohan, get the fuck out of there!'

The Indian contingent began running down the pavement towards the coppers. I pulled Maria Grazia down behind a smashed and empty taxi and bent my chest over her head. What a great first date. I glanced up and saw Bugsy still standing there, arms held above his head like a striker who'd just scored the winning goal.

'Bugsy! Run!' I yelled.

He didn't even look in my direction.

A deafening explosion rocked the entire street. The impact hit Bugsy like a giant invisible fist. He flew backwards through the air and the whole of his body from head to heels bounced and scraped along the tarmac. He lay still, a broken doll. He looked so young like that, so childlike, as he lay there all twisted, his face and arms and clothes all blackened by the blast and bloody where the glass had ripped him.

I was curled up around Maria Grazia. The taxis had sheltered us from the force of the explosion.

'Are you OK?' I asked her.

She lifted her head from my lap and nodded. She unfolded herself from my embrace, got up more easily than I possibly could and then helped me to my feet.

The empty taxis in front of us were blackened and shattered on the side of the blast but there was hardly a nick on the paintwork on the side where we had sheltered. Mohan and his crew had reached the police lines. The distant skinheads who could still stand, gawked back towards us. I couldn't believe it when the coppers started firing off some kind of grenade from fat-barrelled pistols. I didn't know what they were at first. Just white smoke. Then my nose and throat had a weird prickling sensation, but the smoke was drifting away from us.

Gerry, Priest and Morgan rose like battered boxers off the ground.

Gerry shook his head and then screamed at the top of his lungs at the SPG. 'I'm a fucking serviceman. What the fuck do you think you're doing? Get some ambulances here fast.'

But the ambulances were already arriving. Sirens blared up the high street where most of the skins had gone and the slow strobe of the fire engines and ambulances flashed in sequence with the chaos of the flickering firelight. The vehicles trundled over the rubble.

'Davey, let's get out of here,' Maria Grazia said.

Maria Grazia was stunned. Her corkscrew hair was all over the place like a gorgon.

'Wait a minute,' I said.

Up the street, close to Bugsy's fallen body, I saw Steven Bunyan, crawling out backwards from between two taxis. His head hung down from his shoulders at about bumper level. His hands, perversely, gripped the

175

broken glass. He was still drunk out of his mind. In front of me was a piece of a chair leg that had been blasted out of the restaurant. It was there to lay across his neck and wail the living shit out of him and never have anyone come back at me for it. I could have left the bastard dead and got away with it.

What am I? I thought. Predator or victim?

I stepped away from Maria Grazia, not knowing whether to get us out of there, take the opportunity with the chair leg, or help Steven Bunyan get to his feet. I stumbled towards Bunyan. He was kneeling in a pool of his own blood. A splintered piece of door jamb or window frame was stuck deep under his ribcage and had transfixed him like a thick spear right through the flesh of his left-hand side. The blast had torn away the clothes over his gashed stomach. I could see veiny blue loops poking out that must have been his entrails. Blood was pooling back into the gutter. Half his face had been torn away so that you could see the teeth, and more blood rained from his head, a steady shower of bright red. I threw up. Oh God. The poor bastard. Seeing him flayed open like that . . . I mean . . . like Bugsy. I retched again . . . the poor fucking stupid kid. Back then, that's what he'd been. And fucking up his life every day, ever since. I wiped my forehead. Cold sweat. Rest in fucking peace, Bunyan.

Suddenly, that vague ammoniac prickling in my nose and throat became unbearable. My eyes began to burn and tear. I couldn't think. White CS smoke fountained to my right. Black smoke and orange flames belched out of the building on my left. I staggered forward past the wrecked cars. The brace dragged my leg back. I

176

stumbled on the rubble, trying to get free of the hideous vision of Bunyan and the clawing chemicals that were trying to eat into all the membranes in my head and lungs. Tear gas, mucus and curried vomit was choking me. I had my shirt front pulled up to my face but it didn't do any good. I looked for an ambulance man. My arm was stretched out behind me, pointing towards the mess of Bunyan slumped against the tyre of the taxi.

Maria Grazia slipped her arm around me to help me up the street away from the SPG and the CS.

Then I heard the growl of a motorbike. The air was dense. Clouds boiled grey above the high street. A steady blaze of orange flame had engulfed the corner where the restaurant had once been. Firemen now directed jets of thick water into the conflagration. Shards of glass littered the street, some burned deep into the tarmac by the heat and violence of the gas blast. I saw Macky on the bike then as he slowed down, his toes popping through the gears. Throttling back, I saw his hand squeeze and release the easy action of the clutch, the flicker of lights from the ambulances, scurrying medical crews. I turned to look back at the cops. Of course, they'd spotted him. They pointed at him and ran for their cars.

I think Macky recognised me and Maria Grazia as we struggled towards him and away from the gas.

The blue-and-white squad cars, all lights flashing, nearly ran us over as they raced towards Macky. Macky's Kwaka roared forward in a high wheelie and then he hauled the bike around like a wild horse. It snaked back through the hoses, ambulances and emergency crews who were working frantically in the blazing

177

night. The workers leaped away and newly arriving vehicles swerved towards the kerbs as Macky gunned the Kwaka through its gears with two cop cars in wild pursuit. Then they were gone.

Not many skinheads were left now. They had long gone up past the traffic lights below the cenotaph. I saw a blue Chevette driving slowly towards us from among the dazed skinheads. It was my brother Roger and his wife Jill. I couldn't believe it. Where they had appeared from, I didn't know. I didn't care either. I just wanted to get out of there.

'Get in the car,' yelled Roger out the window.

The awful roar of the fire fought the whining sirens. Maria Grazia had the door open and tumbled me into the back seat. She slid in after me and slammed the door on the claws of the tear gas. Jill put the car in reverse and took off zigzagging up the road. She screeched to a halt as Maria Grazia called out, 'There's Morgan and Gerry and Priest.' The three sprinted towards the car. Roger flung the passenger door open and Priest squeezed in beside him. I swung the rear door out at the last second. Gerry and Morgan jumped in the back next to me and Maria Grazia. And we were off again. Backwards through space.

We reached an intersection and Jill hit the brakes, changed into first and put her boot to the boards. She spun the wheel and we shot off the high street.

'Jesus Christ,' groaned Morgan, 'that gas is fucking awful.'

'You're lucky you got out so fast,' said Gerry.

'Roger, I was looking for you earlier,' I croaked.

'Well, here we are, innit?' he said, twisting back

over the front seat, with Priest under his armpit.

'It's a bloody war zone,' said Jill.

'I can't believe this place,' I said. 'What's wrong with everybody? They blew the fucking place up. There's people dead. And Bunyan? Oh Jesus.'

'What happened, Dave?' asked Jill.

'Fucking skinheads. A total fucking riot. The blast smashed Bugsy like an insect. Fucking Bunyan. Gutted. Literally.'

'What about Mohan? And his wife? We were talking about her tonight in the restaurant. She's pregnant.'

'I think they got out. But the fucking restaurant's gone.'

'Insurance'll cover it, mun,' Morgan said, all matter of fact.

'Oh Roger,' Jill said. 'Find out what happened to Mohan and his wife.'

'In the morning,' Roger said.

I was crushed up against Maria Grazia. Her arm was around me. Her breast pressed against me. All the pain of the kicking I'd had was just a dull ache in my ribs, my biceps, my shin. I wanted everything to be all right again. I didn't want to think about what had happened. But it was there like a black hole sucking everything into itself.

'Did you see Macky?' I asked.

'No,' said Morgan.

'He didn't look well,' I said. 'And the coppers took off after him straight away when they saw he was on the Kwaka.'

'He should never have got on that bike,' said Maria Grazia, twisting her head around to look in my face.

'There's no fucking telling him,' said Priest.

The car fell silent till Gerry asked, 'Where we going then?' Ever the fucking pragmatist. Jill had just turned on to the dual carriageway heading south.

'I don't know,' she said. 'Wherever it's safe, innit?'

'Turn off at the next exit,' offered Maria Grazia. 'We can get to my place.'

Up ahead we saw more flashing blue lights. 'Fuck, they're everywhere,' Priest complained. We hadn't even got to the exit we wanted when Jill slowed the car. A black streak twisted down the road in front of us. The police spot lamps shone towards the hard shoulder. They lit up the telegraph pole and the tangle of wires. A hanging bundle. A copper flagged us down frantically but Jill didn't stop. She coasted onwards and braked just before she knocked the copper off his feet. Then Morgan let out a groan. We saw the pale face above the snarl of cables.

'Oh my God.'

'Fuck no.'

3

This is how I see it.

Macky was on the bike. His jeans were soaked through with blood from the knife wound in his side. He wanted to lose the coppers. He whipped the Kwaka into and out of street after street of terraced houses. He checked his mirror each time and each time there was one less, until he was elated to find one solitary Rover hanging on. The driver forced the big car to squeal around corners and stick to Macky's back. On the Kwaka, Macky gunned his way through the night streets. He made for the dual carriageway that led out of the town. He wanted to escape the confines of the streets. He opened the Kawasaki's throttle and accelerated into the darkness. From a side ramp, two panda cars pulled on to the carriageway in front of him. Behind them appeared an old Ford Escort.

A long, black line burned itself into the tarmac, sidewinding down the road. The Kwaka shattered against a tarred telephone pole. Macky pirouetted into the air. There was a snap of the aerial wires and the whistle of whipping steel. The cable wrapped itself around Macky's battered body and jerked it back. With Macky's corpse as a plumb weight, it spiralled insanely around the telephone pole.

Open eyes fixed on his lifelong enemies, the dead biker hung on the splintered trunk.

Chapter 10

1

'You can't go there.'

It was the copper who had flagged us down.

We all piled out of the car. The strobing blue light splashed the tarmac. Behind us, the few cars driving south slowed to a halt and added to the illumination with their headlights.

'Get out of the fucking way,' Morgan yelled.

He ran towards the strung-up body. There was a carload of gypsies beyond the coppers. The doors of their old Ford Escort opened. Two men and one woman got out. The other woman stayed in the driver's seat. One of the men looked in rough shape. His face was all taped up. He dragged his leg and he carried his left shoulder low, his arm limp – like the Hunchback of Notre Dame. The other was a cocky bastard who strutted towards the telegraph pole.

'Get back in the car,' a copper yelled, but the upright gypsy stared him down.

'I'm a fucking witness, ain't I?'

Then he saw Morgan.

I limped forward like a zombie. I heard myself say, 'Macky, mun, Macky, what the fuck are 'ou doin'?'

Maria Grazia hung back with Roger and Jill.

'He bought it this time, butty,' the gypsy said to Morgan.

Morgan's lips pulled back from his teeth. I saw the gypsy's face turn white as he realised he had just stepped into the land of no return. He pulled a knife as Morgan charged towards him. It was a slow-motion movie. The coppers stood by like bewildered extras. Morgan leaped for the gypsy's throat. The knife came up and slid along Morgan's forearm. It gouged a furrow in his jacket sleeve all the way to the biceps. There was a crack and the gypsy's head snapped back under the impact of Morgan's thick skull.

The coppers rushed forward as the fighters lurched towards the hard shoulder and the mangled remains of the Kwaka. The gypsy's arm came back, the knife in his fist. Morgan's fingers dug into the gyppo's neck. The arm swung up and Morgan pushed himself backwards. The knife cut air in front of Morgan's belly but Morgan lost his footing and went down on the oily tarmac.

'Grab 'em,' yelled a sergeant. The coppers rushed forward. The gypsy tried another stab. Morgan rolled over and swung at the gypsy with both feet. The heavy boots smacked into the knifeman's hip and spun him. The gypsy tripped over the wreckage of the Kwaka and sprawled at the feet of Macky's grinning corpse. The cops were on top of him in no time. The gypsy curled into a ball as their clubs came down. Then four coppers jumped on Morgan. They whaled at him with truncheons as he tried to get up.

'Stay down, you bastard.'

Gerry was among them now.

'Morgan, stay quiet.'

He tried to get between his brother and the cops.

'Arrest him,' screeched the fat gypsy woman.

The cops pulled Morgan to his feet. The woman tried to claw at him but two coppers grabbed her arms.

'Hasn't there been enough fucking war?' the hunchback yelled in her face.

A sergeant started shouting. 'I want these animals out of here. I don't care if they both end up dead, I've got enough trouble with this stiff without bothering with a fucking brawl. Get that bastard in his car, and you missus, get him out of here.'

The cops dragged the gypsy fighter to the old Ford and bundled him into the front seat. I knew the woman in the gypsies' car: Clara, Our Lady of the Shadows, ready at the wheel. The taped-face gypsy and the fat woman got in the back. The old Ford started up. The driver pulled on to the open road beyond the mess and peeled off over the tarmac.

'And you,' the sergeant bellowed at Gerry, 'get that fucking yob out of my sight.'

Gerry helped Morgan to his feet.

I stood under the telegraph pole and looked up at Macky.

'Oh God, Macky,' I said.

His body was a broken bloody mess. His eyes were like mirrors in the spotlights. His lips twisted in a dead smirk. Roger, Jill and Priest stayed by the Chevette. Gerry had his arm around Morgan and led him back towards them. Morgan seemed shell-shocked. Maria Grazia came up behind me and touched my shoulder.

'Let's go home, Davey,' she said.

2

We tried to keep our bodies still, seven of us crushed together in the small car. Morgan's arm didn't bleed so badly. Gerry had wrapped a scarf around it. It was one of Jill's that Roger had found on the back seat.

'Look, just take everybody home, Roger,' said Jill. 'I can't cope with this any more.'

Roger had taken the wheel. Jill didn't look comfortable sharing the passenger seat with Priest. He looked out of the window and mumbled, 'What a fucking night, boys. I never thought I'd see anything like this.'

'What are we gonna do about Macky?' Morgan said.

'Sorry, boys. Where do you live, Priest?' Roger asked.

I could feel Morgan tense up next to me. His head twisted around to look out the back window though we'd left the scene of the carnage far behind.

'Take the last exit off the next roundabout, then it's the third street on the right, up the hill.'

'Easy, Morg,' said Gerry. He was so in control of everything. 'Me and you'll go down to the cop shop tomorrow, and see what's happening. Roger, we don't live far from Priest. You can pull back on to Twynrodyn Hill, cut across Balaclava Road by the school, and drop us off on Sherman Street. Then it's a straight run down to the Queen's Café where your lady lives.'

I expect he'd seen a few of his mates buy it in his time.

Roger turned into Inkerman Street. It was so quiet: just cars parked in the night, under street lamps. The pavements drying after the rain. We stopped behind Priest's Ford Transit van. Priest got out. He dug into his pocket for his door key before he slammed the car door. The house was in total darkness, as you'd expect at this time of night.

'I'll ring you tomorrow,' said Priest.

Then he was gone up the steps and into the doorway to his first-floor flat.

We drove on to Morgan's place, the ride only punctuated by monosyllables when Roger asked for directions. Death hung over us. Awkward. Inconvenient. We pulled up outside Morgan's flat.

'See you tomorrow,' said Gerry and he slammed the car door.

Morgan tried to fit the key in his door lock as Roger drove away.

Being less pressed physically, one upon the other, was a relief in some way, but it also seemed to give room for a burgeoning of thought. The what ifs. The if onlys. The desperate and futile attempt to restructure reality to have Macky back. And the Singhs. Even bloody Bunyan. Roger drove on and we reached Maria Grazia's flat. Every muscle and bone was aching and I was glad to get out of the car at last.

'Park over there, Roger,' I said, 'and come up for a minute.'

3

My mouth was dry. Maria Grazia gave me a tumbler of cognac. I'd asked for water. She lit a cigarette, dragged on it, bit at a fingernail, and blew out smoke.

'You all right, Dave?' Roger asked.

Jill was on her feet. She picked up a book off the coffee table. Opened the cover. Put it back before she'd even read the title. 'Oh sorry,' she said, embarrassed to pick up someone else's belongings. Jill obviously didn't want to be thought nosy. She straightened the coasters into a symmetrical layout: two on each side and one at each end of the oval table.

'Well, Rog,' I said, 'my mate's dead, innit? I always thought of Macky as my evil guardian angel. I don't think I've got a chance in this town any more, mun.'

Roger smiled and looked across at Maria Grazia, as if to say, 'What about her then?' He always was the level-headed one. Tried to make light of it. I was angry. What about Macky? And it was early days with Maria Grazia. How could I know what would happen between us?

'Mind if I use the phone, love?' Roger asked Maria Grazia.

She waved the hand with the cigarette. Took another drag.

'Who you calling, Rog?' I asked.

'The old woman,' he said. 'She wanted to know if you were all right.'

'Never!'

I looked at him.

'Aye, she was worried, mun. Saw those skins and all that, earlier on. They went past the house. A mate of the old man's got stabbed as well. That's what we were doing in the car. Come to look for you, innit?'

'Is the old man all right?'

'Oh yeah. I brought him home from the Blaen View. He's fine. Worried about you though.'

'Davey, it's not so strange,' put in Maria Grazia. 'They never stop worrying, do they? Old as you are.'

Maria Grazia looked towards Jill for support. Jill just shook her head.

'Maybe you should have a word with the old lady,' said Roger.

'Fuck no, Rog. Not now. What am I going to say? Hello, Mam? We haven't passed a word for six years and I been out for a night with the boys, like. It was quiet, like, except that my mate Macky got killed.'

Tears welled up. I bit my lip. I was ready to smash my fist through the table. The bruises around my ribs had started to throb again.

'No, Rog,' I said. 'Maybe some other time.' I tried to keep my voice from quavering.

Roger nodded. 'Well, let me call her anyway, to tell her that you're safe. When they see the news in the morning they'll be scared witless, Mam and Dad both.'

I waved at the phone and took a good gulp of brandy. I really wanted fucking water. Why had she given me this?

Roger dialled. Started talking. 'Hallo, Mam, it's me.'

I swung my head from side to side, looked at Jill, then Maria Grazia. I heard Roger say, 'I'm all right. Me and Jill picked Davey up. He's a bit upset, Mam. One of his friends was in a road accident tonight so Davey just wanted to go home.'

My fingers gripped the glass. I felt like ripping the phone cable out. They belonged to another world.

'Yes, yes, Davey's all right. He wasn't in the accident or anything. I took him home.'

Maria Grazia looked at me, her eyes on fire. She didn't have to say anything. I had to calm down. She took another drag on her cigarette. Kept looking at me.

'Yes, you can go to bed,' Roger said. 'There's a hell of a mess in town. Them skinheads. No bother with us though. But I'll tell you about that tomorrow. You'll hear about it soon enough.'

Jill looked at her watch, at Roger, at the door.

'Aye, we're safe and sound. Back home. We're going to bed now.'

I breathed deep and slugged back the brandy.

'Yes, we're fine. No problem. Good night, Mam.'

'So they'll be happy now,' I said with just the faintest trace of bitterness.

'Come on, Dave,' said Roger. 'Give it a rest.'

The booze ate at my liver, got the bile to rise. Roger could see I was close to apoplectic.

'Don't get fucking nasty now,' said Roger.

He was my brother – a real one – fucking right – all right – I couldn't stay mad at him, could I? He'd just dragged me off the street. Got me here to Maria Grazia's place safe and sound.

'Sorry, Rog,' I told him, 'I'm no good at the domestic stuff. You know that.'

'Rog, it's awful late,' said Jill.

You couldn't blame her for wanting to get out of there. Too much madness for one night.

'We better be going, Dave,' said Roger.

I nodded. 'All right,' I said.

Maria Grazia put out her cigarette.

'Hey, thanks, Roger, for coming down looking for us. Thanks, Jill.'

She got up and kissed Jill on the cheek. Dark-haired woman in black, blonde woman in white. Jill moved towards the door. Maria Grazia stood in the middle of the room.

'I'll call you up tomorrow, Rog,' I said.

As we stood at the door of the flat, Maria Grazia slipped her arm around my waist, and we watched Roger and Jill go down the narrow stairs.

'Night, both,' called Roger, and the door slammed shut behind them.

4

Mother Maeve put down the telephone. Ben picked up the crockery from the coffee table and laid it in the sink. They went upstairs, used the bathroom and proceeded to bed as usual. Maeve curled up close to Ben. That night she dreamed that she was praying her thanks to the Virgin of Dalkey at the very shrine where the shepherd had seen her. Mrs Daunt lifted her eyes and there before her was a figure dressed in blue and white, a rosary twined in her joined hands. The apparition glowed out of the depths of a crystal cave. It was surrounded by lilies. (She told Ben and Roger all about it, convinced of immaculate intervention.)

Two streets away, Gripper was preparing to sleep on Linda's parents' sofa. They had just had more comfortable sex on the living-room floor, as quietly as possible, so that they didn't wake up Linda's parents.

'It's funny, innit, Grip. I never thought that going on a rampage would get you out, but it did, didn't it?'

'I suppose it did, Lind. I wonder what they're doing now, all the Shop Boys?'

'Probably going home. It's late, innit?'

'Yeah, I expect so,' yawned Gripper.

'See you in the morning, Grip.'

'Night, Lind.'

'Night.'

And where was PC Phillips?

He sat in the waiting room of the Prince Charles Hospital casualty department. The place was packed with medical staff, battered policemen and injured skinheads. The young copper was waiting for an X-ray report on Sergeant Thomas, whose head had been split open by a piece of paving stone.

There were four SPG men there too. They grabbed each skinhead who was fixed up, and after a brief interview, charged them with riotous assembly, malicious damage and anything else they could pin on them. The parents of some of the kids were there, dragged out of bed at three in the morning. The men were dishevelled, some of them reeking of booze, and the women were hollow-eyed from lack of sleep. A fat woman with her hair in curlers berated her brooding husband.

'It's your bloody fault! You let him get away with murder. You should have used the bloody belt on him some more. He always quietened down after you gave him some of that.'

PC Phillips wondered disconsolately if he was going to have to step in to prevent a public outbreak of domestic violence. The young copper was tired. Looking across this disaster area of torn and bloody bodies, he wished that he had never got out of his car when that one small stone had bounced off the roof.

5

In the courtyard behind the Queen's Café, pre-dawn starlight made Christmas among the budding twigs. Rebirth of the green god. I turned away from the bathroom window and went to the sink, washed my hands, then my face. My mouth was coated with coarse grit. My bones and muscles were on fire. The scrape on my shin burned like hell. I took Maria Grazia's toothbrush and scraped at my teeth, my gums, the roof of my mouth, my tongue. I rinsed and spat. Thin line of blood in the saliva. There were some aspirin in the medicine cabinet and a glass. I swallowed three tablets followed by a pint of water. Maria Grazia was still asleep.

I went into the living room and found her shawl. I twisted it around my hips. My little black book was in my jacket pocket. I wanted to write something for Macky but nothing came in words. Images of his face looking down on the cops, then the memories of making love with Maria Grazia in the dark grew more persistent. Some kind of defence mechanism, I thought. Maybe Macky would have preferred it that way. I scratched at the paper, hatch marks, but then began to draw a passable sketch of Maria Grazia. I thought of the party. I'd promised her a poem. Some day, I thought, I'll write one for her. And for Macky, an epic. Maria Grazia came into the room, still naked. The sun was up. So was my cock seeing her like that, the tits, the belly, the bush.

'What you doing, Davey?'

I waved the pen around. 'I'm trying to write a poem or something, but the words won't come out.'

'Hey, that's me,' she said.

She leaned over and kissed me on the lips. In the dark room, her glow; outside in the bright daylight, the shadow of Macky's death. Then the phone rang.

Maria Grazia picked it up. I saw from her face that it was one of the boys, and then she handed it to me.

'It's Priest,' she said.

'Hello, Priest, what's going on?'

'Morgan called me. Some young copper came for him this morning. They needed someone to identify the body officially. There's no family, like.'

'Where's Morgan now?' I asked.

'He's down there. Doing the business. I said I'd meet him in the Rails this afternoon.'

'I'll be there,' I said and put the phone down. I wanted to make love to Maria Grazia again. I had always been pulled in two directions. Out with the boys or in with a woman. Thanatos and Eros having a fight. I was glad I was on the right side this once.

6

Maria Grazia had to take care of the café. Saturdays were always busy and her parents were away. I went to the Rails. I told her that I'd call later. When I got to the pub, Morgan's face was all lines and shadows. It was as if something was eating him from the inside out, determined to leave him an empty shell. Gerry turned his pint in his hands:

'He would have wanted to go this way,' he said.

Nobody said a word, but Gerry seemed determined to get us to talk. 'What shall we do for the funeral then, boys?'

'We'll have six black horses with tall black plumes. They can pull a mahogany wagon,' said Priest. 'And there'll be an escort of a hundred and fifty Hell's Angels on motorbikes; and a New Orleans marching band.'

There were a few smiles at that.

'Someone should get his dog and his shotgun,' said Morgan.

We decided to go up the mountain in Priest's Transit van. He had driven down and he was parked behind the Rails. We drove up through the backstreets. A fire smouldered outside the front door of Macky's shack. Half of the dog's body was still attached to the line: the front half. The back end seemed to have been cut off. I was glad that Maria Grazia wasn't with us. Morgan unhooked the snap from its collar and, bare-handed, scooped the dog's remains into a wooden fruit crate that he found in the kitchen. He placed the box of charred hair and entrails inside the front door of the shack.

Morgan broke open the cupboard and took out Macky's shotgun and cartridges. He put them in the back of Priest's van and then went round the back of the building to the lean-to. He found a gallon can of petrol in there. He spattered the contents all over the two rooms and then threw in a match. There was a whoosh, and a wall of orange flame leaped up from the wooden floor. In no time, the place was ablaze.

Priest was horrified. He obviously wanted to get out of there as fast as possible. He didn't have to wait long.

'That was Macky's place,' said Morgan. 'Nobody should have it after him.'

We piled into the van, and headed for town.

7

RACE RIOT ERUPTS IN VALLEYS TOWN — THREE DEAD, SCORES INJURED

CHASE DEATH IN VALLEYS RIOT

The billboards greeted our return. There were 'in-depth' reports in the *South Wales Echo* trying to get to the bottom of neo-Nazi violence. A special article told how the ringleader of the rioters had attempted to escape on a stolen motorcycle, and met his death trying to avoid the pursuit of brave coppers risking life and limb to bring him in.

Who gave them that line of shit, I don't know.

The television crews were out in force as we drove by. They pointed their cameras at the black remains of the Taj Mahal curry house and the looted window of Amrit's Discount Stereo Centre.

Back in the pub the news was on. Superintendent Sykes praised his men's bravery in the face of wanton violence and told how he was recommending decoration for the men injured in the line of duty; and especially for one PC Phillips, who had displayed extraordinary courage in the rescue of the injured Sergeant Thomas from under a hail of bricks and bottles.

'No,' he said, 'nothing my men could have done would have saved any of the three who died. The investigation is continuing to bring the ringleaders to justice.'

That night riots broke out in Southall, Brixton, Birmingham, Halifax and Leeds. Some were billed as protests against neo-Nazis; some as right-wing, copycat skinhead riots; some as protests against police brutality in black neighbourhoods; and some didn't seem to have any reason at all, except for the desire to have a bloody good riot.

The Prime Minister spoke, and the Home Secretary, the head of the Police Federation and the Leader of the Opposition. All of them condemned the 'senseless violence', and assured the public that it would not be tolerated. None of them sounded as if they had a clue what was going on in the streets and the housing estates. There were no pretty pictures.

8

Gerry had seen to all the arrangements. Macky was laid out in the funeral home. He did not rise on Easter Sunday but the mortician had done a great job. Macky in a suit: velvet collar, nice drape, the tattoos on his neck visible under the open collar. The Monday, being a bank holiday, was also no good for a funeral. On the Tuesday, then, we all sat in the parlour to wait for the hearse. Priest went over to the open coffin. In his hand he had a small, square envelope that was wrapped up in a crossed pattern of five coloured threads. He slipped it under Macky's shirt.

'Some Hindu thing, is it?' I said.

'Buddhist,' he said.

'What good will that do him?' I asked.

Priest shrugged. 'Maybe he'll find himself in some kind of Valhalla where he can fuck and fight to his heart's content.'

'Not exactly Heaven or Hell then, Priest?' I said.

'I never thought it was as simple as that,' he said.

'Just as well,' I told him. 'I hope Macky's all right.'

'Me too,' Priest said. 'Where's Maria Grazia?'

'She'll be here in a minute.'

Maria Grazia came in then. Dressed in black. She looked gorgeous. It was time to go to the cemetery on Macky's last ride. It was his day, after all. Despite our fantasies we settled for what we could afford: a plain pine box and Effy Griffiths' hearse. Morgan did hire the Colliers' Brass Band of Deep Navigation Mine. Macky's father had been a miner when he was alive. Mourners were few and far between, just us. There were a few reporters and photographers. They kept back from us and didn't ask any questions. It was cold and wet as we marched into the cemetery. It would have been nice to have a few of those IRA boys in dark glasses and berets to fire a volley over the grave but Gerry might have been a bit miffed at that.

The brash blast of the brass band crashed sharp against the damp air. Morgan, Gerry, Priest, Gary Taft the Lorries, Berwyn Evans the Brickie and me supported the pall upon our shoulders. It was hard for me to keep in step. I was still aching all over from the beating I'd got. We brought the coffin to the graveside and laid it on the red ropes. We gripped the thick cords and swung Macky's box over the earthen hole. It wasn't that heavy. As we lowered the coffin into the grave, the skinny gypsy woman came in through the cemetery gates. She was carrying a single white lily. Maria Grazia looked shocked. I saw Morgan stiffen – momentarily halting the play of the rope and causing the coffin to tilt. Then we let the bier slide easy on to the earth. The gypsy woman came right up to the foot of the grave, Clara, Our Lady of Shadows. She tossed her lily on to the coffin.

Effy Griffiths, the funeral director, asked if someone was going to say a few words. Priest nodded.

'This is a poem by W.B. Yeats,' Priest said.

And he began: '*A man, violent and famous, strode among the dead . . .*'

As Priest intoned the poem, I slid my arm around Maria Grazia. She squeezed my hip above the brace. She was still with me. Like a dream. All around, the green mountains were dark and scarred with the black of unreclaimed slag heaps, thick cloud hanging low over the desolate valley and a fine drizzle starting to fall. I pulled up the collar of my leather jacket with my left hand, kept the right around Maria Grazia.

Three crows flapped noisily past and landed on the fenceposts beside us. The night-black birds tilted their heads so that their sideways eyes pierced the west.

Their voices almost human, they cawed an occult eulogy.